DEADLY SAI

Book Two

By J&L Brown

Printed in the United States of America

First Printing, 2019

Cover Design by Diana TC, triumphbookcovers.com

Print Edition ISBN: 978-0-578-55700-7
Ebook ISBN: 978-0-578-55778-6

Table of Contents

To our family
For your love, support, feedback, and being
our biggest cheerleaders.

This is not a standalone book, please read Deadly Sai Book One before continuing!

Chapter 1

Kamari

You know the drill. After my job is completed, I hit the bar before going back home, but since there are no bars in this God-forsaken town, I go back to my motel, pack up and check out. I figured I might as well drive back toward the airport to find a bar. My flight is in the a.m., so I'll get a room as well for one night.

***

After checking into the new hotel, I put my bag in the room and turn on the TV. The local news is on with some type of weather alert. I sit on the bed to watch and dammit . . there's a sandstorm coming this way from the west and all flights going west are canceled until further notice while they keep an eye on the storm. Well, I guess my drink can wait, nothing like an unexpected break in the middle of nowhere. Geez!!

Shit, now I'm kicking myself for not bringing my Switch. Who am I kidding? I'm never anywhere long enough to actually play. I bet you if I bring it from this point forward I'll never use it. I guess I'll go for a jog. There are more things to do now that I'm closer to the airport. I'll hit the bar after my run. The bar is connected to the airport so they'll have updates regarding the storm and flights. Better to get the updates there than waiting for the news to get it wrong.

***

I order my usual, down the shot and sip on my white Russian. After a few sips, this guy sits next to me but doesn't say a word. . . *that's different*. He orders a rum & Coke with a Bud Light chaser and a shot of whiskey. I watch him out of the corner of my eye; he downs the shot, swallows more than half the beer

1

and then starts on the drink. Must've had a rough day. I look at him and WOW, he's fuckin' gorgeous. I mean he can make you cum in your panties just by looking at him. Not just his face either, you can tell he's ripped underneath his clothes as well and now I can even smell him; it's like musk, no, no. It's like that Opium cologne that's hard to find and it smells like pheromones on steroids, Jesus! Then I start to get offended that he hasn't said anything to me yet. I mean, no guy EVER just sits next to me and doesn't say anything. He must be playing with me or something. Now he's realizing I'm staring at him, *which is something I don't do*, and I must have a look on my face because he starts talking.

"Is there a problem?"

"What?"

"Well, you're staring at me, so I say again. Is there a problem?"

"No, well yeah. You've been sitting next to me for a bit and you haven't said a word. I mean most guys would've said something to me by now."

"Well, #1 I'm not most guys, and #2 I'm talking to you now. Feel better? Can I go back to my drink now?"

I squint my eyes at him because now he's pissing me off. "Come on buddy look at me." At this point, I am actually acting like one of those women on 'The Price Is Right' showing him the merchandise. "I can never sit at the bar without being accosted."

"Well someone's full of themselves." He turns back to his drink and continues sipping.

Oh my God, this nigga is actually ignoring me. That never happens and I'm not even sure how to respond to it. I turn back to my drink and start tapping the counter out of frustration. I turn back to him to say something, but nothing comes out. Before I turn back to my drink again, I can see him smirking. He's actually fucking smirking. "What's so funny?"

"You seem really bothered by the fact I didn't stroke your ego. Isn't that usually a guy thing?"

"Are you serious!?"

"What did you think I was going to say?" [Laughing]—"Did you think I was going to apologize for not hitting on you?"

Then I actually thought about how I sounded. "Oh my God! I'm sorry. I can't even explain why I'm acting like this." I look into his eyes and they are the prettiest shade of caramel I've ever seen in my life.

"No problem. I guess we're both having one of those days." He pays for his drinks, leaves extra for the bartender, and even pays for mine before getting up and walking out the door. Before I knew it, I was out the door behind him grabbing his hand.

"Wait. Let me make it up to you."

"Like I said, it's no problem. There's nothing to atone for."

"Ok, then let me be direct. What does a girl have to do to go out with you?"

"Well that depends on what she's looking for."

"You seem like a guy worth knowing." He then steps toward me really, really close, I mean close enough for me to smell him again, his scent filling my nose and making me tingling all over. He grabs my chin with the lightest touch lifting my head slightly and looks into my eyes. The caramel color of his eyes almost seem to glow when he says,

3

"I don't do drive-byes. You're not emotionally ready for me darlin'."

"Say what?!"

"I can read people pretty well. I can tell by your eyes you're a loner, been one for a while. You're detached from everything and everyone. That makes you someone who likes to be in control or feel you have to be in order to feel safe."

"And you can tell that just by looking into my eyes?"

"Pretty much. Even if I went out with you, you probably wouldn't tell me anything about yourself or lie about it straight out. So what's the point?"

"Well most guys don't care about me, they just wanna hit it and bounce."

"And clearly you're used to that type of guy. Like I said before, I'm not most guys. What's your name sweetheart?"

"Kamari." *Shit!* It left my lips before I could even think.

"Wow, that's beautiful. That's Japanese for moon right?"

"Ho—, how do you know that?"

"I read. Now that I look at you more closely I can see your Japanese features, the shape of your eyes, your cheekbones. You're as beautiful as your name. Someone as beautiful as you should never be alone."

"So what are you going to do about that . . . ? I don't even know your name."

"I'm JT."

4

"That's not the name your momma gave you; those are initials."

"You're right. It's Jordan."

"Well Jordan, you gonna help me with my loneliness?"

"No one calls me Jordan. And to answer your question, that's not up to me Mari. Can I call you that?"

"Hmm . . . no one has ever called me that before. It sounds nice when you say it, so yeah. And since no one calls you Jordan, it must be meant for me alone to use. Tell me Jordan, what's a girl gotta do to get you to assist her?"

"Tell you what, hand me your phone. I'm gonna type in my number, the hotel and room number where I'm staying. Come by tomorrow night around 7 p.m. if you want. Think about it first though. If you don't show up nothing lost, but if you do you might be in for a surprise."

"Why do you say that?"

"Like I said, I don't do drive-byes. You're a loner and you're probably thinking, you'll just get what you *think* you want and leave, but I can tell you're tired of being alone. When's the last time someone took care of you Mari and I mean really cared for you? You don't have to answer. As a matter of fact, if you show up I'll give you everything you need and find out enough about you without asking any questions."

"You're kidding me?"

"Goodnight Mari. Maybe I'll see you tomorrow?" And he kisses me on my forehead, my frickin' forehead but the heat from his lips I felt all the way down to my toes. What the fuck is happening to me???

Chapter 2

JT

I get up early to drive to Supai where the last homicide took place. I pull into a dirt road where a uniform is directing authorized personnel to the scene. When driving up to the house, I wonder if the perp came during the day or at night. It's an isolated place so the time of day probably didn't matter. In looking at the outside scene, it was a great idea for me to get here before the sandstorm, as the window is busted out completely and the storm would've contaminated everything. I meet up with the local sheriff, Richard Franklin. He walks up to my car as the uniform radioed ahead to tell him I had arrived.

"Morning. JT right?"

"Yes sir!"

"I'm Sheriff Franklin. Sorry to have you come all this way, but I hear you're the man to call for weird things such as this."

I exit the car. "No problem Sheriff, I'm happy to help. What information do you have for me so far?" I ask as I shake his hand.

"Well, honestly I can't tell who did what. The entire house is tore up like a brawl took place. Only the husband and wife were found, so there was definitely a third person but by the looks of everything I can't really tell what happened."

"Were there two victims?"

"Oh sorry, yes and no. Looks like the husband was beating the wife on a regular basis. She was barely breathing when we found her; she's at the local hospital. The husband is your victim and if you ask me, he got off easy. Here." He hands me photos taken of the scene. "These are the photos of the wife before she left in an ambulance. They include photos of where we found her before the paramedics moved her."

"Jesus, and she survived?"

"Exactly! The husband got off easy. I'll let you do your thing but I'm here if you have any questions, not that I could help."

"You'd be surprised, walk with me."

I look inside the house from outside of the broken window, the point of entry. It was definitely broken from the outside, but the glass is almost on the other side of the room. That took a lot of force. I ask the sheriff, "Was there some sort of tool left behind that broke the window? I'm surprised how far the shards of glass made it into the room."

"Yeah, I noticed that too but there was nothing around the window or the house that looked like it broke the glass."

We walk inside. I place the photo of the wife in front of the couch where she previously laid by the phone. The husband's body is still in the room. I take a look at the phone and ask, "What's with the blood on the phone?"

"Now that's the strangest thing. The person who killed the husband called 9-1-1 for the wife and placed the phone by her body before leaving. So I guess after they killed him," then we walked over to the husband's body, "you can see whatever they used to poke him with, they used to dial on the phone."

"They didn't use a tool to poke him; those are finger strikes my friend."

"Finger strikes? What the hell are you talking about?"

I stooped down over the body and looked at each strike on the torso, and they are in the same position of my victim from

7

the alley but these are more violent as the skin was penetrated and bled. It looks almost like someone burned him with a cigar or something. "Well, I have another case like this one, just not to this degree. Some guy was 'poked' as you put it in the same manner, but these strikes broke the skin making the victim bleed. The strikes paralyze the diaphragm making it impossible for the victim to breathe. So in essence, he suffocated."

"You're shittin' me? So you saying some karate person with the Kung Fu grip bust through that der winda, karate chopped the husband to death, dialed 9-1-1 with the same bloody fingers and walked out? That sounds like a bad joke!"

"Yeah, seems like a lot of my cases are turning out that way. Looking around the place, I would say the husband and wife were fighting, and the perp was watching at that window. When the husband and wife ended up in this room, they had to have seen something that made them save the wife. I mean, if the husband was beating her on the regular, I can understand taking a hit out on him. Looking at the photos of the wife, she has a lot of bruising, like it's been going for weeks, maybe even months or years. You can see the marks around her neck, so maybe the husband was choking her. I would say that's when the perp busted in and took the husband out. Hmm . . . considering the blows kept him from breathing, they in essence inflicted the same pain he inflicted on his wife. A killer with compassion, that's different. Did the wife say anything before she was taken to the hospital?"

"No, she never came to before leaving and word has it she's in a medically-induced coma; it looks like she'll pull through, but it will be a while."

"Well, let's do a probe on the wife's family and the husband's just in case. I would think someone wanted to save her from her husband and paid to have him knocked off. I'm just guessing at this point."

"Wow, you're really sumthin!"

"Naw Sheriff, just been at it, unfortunately, a very long time. Here's my card, call me when the wife wakes up and give me the details on the family members when you get it.

"Will do JT! I appreciate your assistance."

***

I prepare for Mari's arrival because it'll shock me if she doesn't show up but I want to be prepared anyway. I pick up scented candles, massage oil, bubble bath. I even go out on a limb and pick up peach and apple Sake (not knowing which one she likes) along with fresh-made sushi and sashimi (*there's no way she doesn't eat it with her background*). I found a restaurant that ships in the fish fresh every other day and I got the last of it as the restaurant is closing a few days early before the storm hits. No condoms. She doesn't know it yet, but tonight is all about her.

Chapter 3

Kamari

I laid awake the entire night; I mean not a wink of sleep. I never go sleepless, ever! All I could do was think about everything Jordan said to me, how he could read me just by looking into my eyes. Hmm . . . maybe the eyes are the window to the soul. There's something about him, I can't tell what but whatever it is, it feels like it'll have me spilling my guts like I'm in a confessional or something. I just blurted my name out as soon as he asked; I'm still shocked about that one. I've never told anyone my real name, why did I feel the need to give it to him so freely? I find it amazing that he just doesn't want to hit it and quit it like all the rest, that way we both get what we want and go our separate ways satisfied. Of course no one has ever cared for me other than family; I can't get close to anyone, not in my line of work. Am I tired of being alone? Probably. Is my going to Jordan tonight the first step in changing that or will I even want to? I guess I'll find out.

***

I arrive at Jordan's door and knock right at 7 p.m. He greets me with a killer smile. Geez, can this guy do anything and not look so damn good?

"Hey Mari, come on in."

"Evening Jordan, by the looks of things you were expecting me?"

"To be honest, it was really only a 50/50 chance but it pays to be prepared."

"Oh my, you went all out. Did you really go out and buy me the triple S threat?

"The triple S threat?

"Yeah, sashimi, sushi and Sake?"

"Sure did, I wanted you to feel as comfortable as possible."

"And what flavor Sake did you get?"

"Well I didn't want to guess on that one, so I bought both apple and peach, but I warmed the peach."

The smile on my face was hurting my cheeks, "Peach is my favorite. How did you know to warm it?"

"I told you before, I read. No worries, it's not too hot but the food and drink come after."

"After what exactly? Jordan, clearly we're not going to be doing what I think, so why don't you enlighten me."

"Nervous?"

"Honestly, a little."

"I bet that's never happened before huh?"

"Are you going to do that all night?"

"Do what?"

"Tell me what I'm thinking and feeling."

"Why yes, yes I am. And the fact that you made the conscious decision in this moment to stay all night brings a smile to my face."

"You still haven't said what we're doing, besides eating later."

"Fair enough. First, I'm going to blindfold you."

"Nope, I'm out!"

"Come on, don't be scared. Would you feel more comfortable if I tell you sex is off the table?"

"Now I know you're joking. Isn't that why I'm here?"

"Mari, we never discussed particulars. I can tell by your reaction you're used to being in control, pretty much dominant. I promise I won't do anything to you that makes you physically uncomfortable; emotionally, I may push a boundary or two, nothing you can't handle I'm sure. I won't hurt you Mari."

"Ok. I'm taking a big leap here."

"I know you are and I won't take that for granted. I promise. Now come with me."

Chapter 4

JT

I take Mari to the bathroom where the scented candles are already lit and the bubble bath is ready. I clip up her hair and start to remove her clothes.

"You can ask me any question you wish, but know if you ask it I have the right to know the same about you. So, if it's not something you want to share with me about yourself, then don't ask me. Mari, I'll know if you're lying."

"Really?"

"You can test it out if you wish."

"No, I believe you. Can we compromise on the blindfold? How about I keep my eyes closed giving me the option to open them if I feel I need to. I'm not ready for that level of vulnerability."

"Okay, I can agree to that." I finish undressing her and find myself perusing her entire beautiful body.

"Are you ogling me?"

"Not at all, I'm admiring and kicking myself for taking sex off the table." She giggles. "That's a beautiful laugh, sounds like you don't do it often enough."

"Oh my God, it's like you're psychic or something. I guess I don't have much to laugh about."

I give no response to her comment on purpose as I want her to feel comfortable talking to me. I guide Mari into the tub and I can tell she is starting to feel nervous again. She pops one eye open, seeing I'm still dressed and asks,

"You're not joining me?"

"No, I will be bathing you love. Tonight is all about you."

"Really? Why?"

"Because sometimes it feels nice to be cared for. You seem like you can use a lot of it."

"Jordan?"

"Yeah."

"If I forget to tell you, I really appreciate what you're doing for me tonight."

       I grab her chin and kiss her lightly on the lips. I lean her head back on the bath pillow and start bathing her. Her face takes on a completely different look from yesterday when I met her. Like her first wall has been knocked down. I wash her entire body with an occasional lingering around her nipples, just for fun. Her breathing picks up a bit.

"Jordan, do you have any siblings?"

"No, I'm an only child. You?"

"Same."

"Are your parents living?"

"No. My dad died at the ripe old age of 78 and my mom of a broken heart 3 months later. You?"

"My parents died in car accident, mudslide actually, after being caught in a typhoon in Japan."

After several long minutes of silence, I can hear Mari's stomach grumble. "I can hear your stomach. You ready for some food?"

"Yes." I help Mari out of the tub, dry her off, wrap her in a robe, and let her hair down when I notice a single tear running down her face. I wipe it away and pull her in for a hug. She grips me, hard. Losing one's parents can definitely make anyone feel totally alone at any age. Just speaking from personal experience.

Chapter 5

Kamari

       I feel Jordan wipe away a tear on my face that I didn't even feel fall from my eye, but just the small mention of my parents had me missing them terribly. At that moment, he pulled me in for a hug and it felt like . . . home. I put my arms around him and hugged him hard, not realizing how bad I needed to be held, nothing sexual, just comfort. He guides me out of the bathroom and back to the table.

"You can open your eyes for now babe. I'm not sure if you'd appreciate me feeding you."

I laugh, "Hmmm. . . yeah, the image in my head doesn't work out too well. Why did you hug me?"

"Because you needed it?"

"Okay let me re-phrase. Why did you feel I needed a hug?"

"I know how I felt when my parents died. Seems like regardless of age, you feel like an orphan when you lose them both. I had aunts, uncles, cousins nearby so got lots of love and lots of hugs, and I was already grown when they passed. I think it was hard for you to mention your parents; you probably never shared that with anyone, and I appreciate you sharing it with me. When I saw the tear on your cheek I felt for you. A hug was the only thing that seemed right in the moment."

"You're right. I've never told anyone about my parents. I'm not even sure why I mentioned them to you."

"Maybe you felt I would understand once I told you how my parents died. You might not have told me at all if one or both were still living."

I begin eating my sashimi and I can feel another tear stream down my face. I'm always sentimental when eating this type of meal but I guess after our previous conversation, I'm a little more sensitive. Jordan gets up from his seat, walks over to me and wipes it away. He kisses me on the top of my head and goes over to the bed and I ask,

"What are you doing?"

"I'm getting the bed ready? How's the Sake?"

"Blissfully good, and I thought you said no sex tonight."

"I know; I'm going to give you a massage."

"One with a happy ending?"

"Of course!"

"And you want nothing from me, at all?"

"Mari, I'm getting plenty from you. You just don't see it."

Chapter 6

JT

       This poor girl, she seems to feel truly alone. It was a really big step for her to share the information about her parents. I wonder what else she'll open up about. After she finishes her food, she closes her eyes again and I bring her to the bed by carrying her.

"Whoa, I wasn't expecting that" she says when I lifted her off the floor (*she weighs next to nothing*), and then I can feel her nuzzling into my chest. I hold her in my arms for a few more seconds before placing her softly on her feet to remove the robe and have her lie down. "Lie down for me. I wanna start on your back first." I pin her hair out of the way again and grab the heated oil. I start with her shoulders, which are no surprise tense, moving all the way down her arms to her fingertips on both sides.

"Oh my God, that feels sooo good! Let me guess you read a book?"

I chuckle. "Something like that."

"Do you treat all your girlfriends like this?"

"Let's just say, they get what's needed."

"And yet you are still single. . ."

"Just haven't found *the one* I guess."

"And are you looking for *the one*?"

"Nope, I read somewhere when you look, one never finds. Don't make me break into a rendition of Heavy D."

"You're adorable."

"You ticklish?"

"What? No, why?"

Just then I test her denial and run my finger quickly right down the middle of her foot. She gasps.

"I thought you weren't ticklish."

"I thought I wasn't. Maybe I subconsciously always block it out and you've chiseled away my defenses."

"Hmm, all part of my master plan. I'm going to start at your feet now, don't kick me since you obviously have no control down here." She laughs again. I spread her legs slightly so I can have access to where her thighs meets her hips. As I move up her legs her breathing changes.

"Jordan?"

"Yeah."

"You do realize what you're doing to me right?"

"Absolutely!"

"And you're still not going to fuck me?"

"Mari, when you let me, I won't fuck you at all. I'll make love to you."

"What makes you think I don't want you to right now?"

"Because when I finish with you tonight, you'll need your rest. You're wound pretty tight, when I get you totally relaxed, you'll be too spent to do anything but sleep." I tap her ass lightly right on her tattoo. "Cute tattoo. Rollover for me."

"Thanks, do you know what they are? Wait, don't answer that. I'm going to assume you do."

"And you would be right." I begin rubbing her thighs, dragging my thumbs in the crevice where her panty line would be while pressing firmly on the sides of her hips. I tap her arms and tell her "put your hands behind your head."

She laughs again, "You sounded like a cop when you said that."

"I guess anyone would saying that line specifically." I straddle her hips and press my hard-on right against her V. Not sure if I'm punishing her or myself with that move. I massage her shoulders again, before straddling her thighs so I can massage her stomach, which I must say are the best set of abs I've ever seen on a woman. I work the sides of her waist and come up and around her perky breasts where her nipples have pebbled . . . hard.

"Jordan?"

"Yeah."

"You're driving me insane already."

"Patience grasshopper."

She laughs.

Chapter 7

Kamari

   The instant Jordan straddled me and I felt his hard-on I wanted him inside me. He has rubbed on my body all frickin' night and no sex?! I think I'm gonna die. Patience, is he kidding? He moved from on top of me and laid beside me. He grabbed my right leg and placed it over his, opening my legs and then I feel his warm mouth on my nipple and OH! MY! GOD! He runs his fingers between my folds and begins to rub my clit. Jesus. .I can cum right now. I have no control over my body. I can't think straight at all. The sounds coming from my throat don't even sound like me. He brings me to the brink within a few minutes and then stops.

I open my eyes and look at him. "Oh God, what are you doing?" My voice is beyond breathy.

"You think all this work and I'm going to let you cum on just my fingers. Think again."

   Jordan moves slowly between my legs, kneeling. He places each arm under the bend of my knees and drags me back to his. He then steps off the bed, kneeling to the floor and dragging me one last time until I can feel his hot breath on my pussy. He presses my legs wide and slides his fingers inside me. I arch my back at the feel. He strokes my walls with his fingers several times.

"Damn baby, you're so wet." I can't even speak at this point, I just moan as he adds another finger, curling them just the right way and I sit up.

"Oh God, Jordan. I'm not going to last, you've got to go slower."

"Mari, I'm not even going that fast. I think you're just completely relaxed, so you have nothing left to fight with. So don't. Just enjoy it."

And with those words, I lean back and close my eyes again still breathing heavily. He places his fingers back inside me but this time he licks my clit as well. The double assault is insane. I can't breathe, I mean I'm breathing, gasping for air but it seems like I can't get enough. Then he starts sucking on me and I think my legs are completely in the air now on their own. He feels so good my body has a mind of its own. I find my hands on his head feeling him bob up and down on my clit, now adding a third finger and driving me crazy. I'm grinding on his face with my legs in the air and oh God, "Jordan, mmmm, don't stop, don't stop, mmmm, mmmm. OH GOD!" I came so hard my nipples hurt and I mean I'm still cuming, it just won't stop and then he sucks on me . . . hard, and I cum again. And just when I think he's done, he sticks a finger in my forbidden hole and now it's a goddamn triple assault, he won't stop and I can't even protest because it feels so fucking good and not even a heartbeat later I'm cuming again. Shit, I got nothing left. I don't think I've ever cum that hard before in my life.

Chapter 8

JT

I get up from the floor looking at Mari; she's so beautiful, breathing hard, still with her eyes closed. I run to the bathroom to get the shower going for me and bring back a hot towel to wipe her off. I pick her up in my arms, and place her back near the head of the bed with a pillow under her head. I cover her with the blanket. I go to walk away and she grabs my hand.

"Where're you going?"

"I'll be right back. Gonna take a quick shower." I kiss the top of her head, and she lets me go.

I take a 10-minute shower with half of it cold as fuck. I dry off and hop in the bed right next to Mari, skin on skin. She seemed to be sleeping deeply but stirred as I move next to her. As soon as I lie on my back, she's right on my chest, her ear to my heartbeat, one leg across my waist, and a death grip you wouldn't believe, and for some reason it feels like the best place in the world to be. It's the best sleep I've had in a very, very long time and my guess is she'll tell you the same thing.

***

Surprisingly enough, I wake early in the morning when I no longer feel Mari's death grip. She's moaning, nightmare maybe, nope, nope, not a nightmare as she has changed positions and although she is still wrapped around me, she now has a slightly less death grip (*thank God*) of my dick in her hand. She's definitely dreaming, about me and last night I hope. Shit, the pressure on my dick is fuckin' amazing. I want to wake her but damn you're not supposed to wake people when they're vividly dreaming. . .right? Wait, wait that's sleepwalkers, *shitshitshit*. I can't think with her stellar grip on my dick. She begins kissing my shoulder up to my neck, stroking me the entire time. Fuck!! I didn't plan for this, not that I'm complaining. I gently rub her head and call her name softly to wake her "Mari." She smiles but doesn't open her eyes. "Mari," she kisses my neck and says,

"Make love to me Jordan." Shit, is she still dreaming?

"Mari, wake up."

"Hmmm . . . hey. Good morning? Did I wake you?"

"Sssss, considering where your hand is, yeah."

"I was dreaming about you and last night."

"Yeah, I gathered that. Ya know, you talk in your sleep."

"Really, what did I say?" Mind you she is still stroking me through the entirety of our conversation.

"You asked me to make love to you."

"And what're you waiting for? I'm not leaving until I have you Jordan. Sex being off the table was last night. I want you Jordan, *please*."

I reach for the drawer of the nightstand, but she stops me.

"I want all of you Jordan, no barriers."

"You sure?"

She rolls onto her back pulling me with her. I look into her eyes and the loneliness of them has dissipated. They seem to almost sparkle as she looks at me. It's the most beautiful thing I've ever seen. I spread her legs and slowly breach her entrance. She digs her nails into my back. "Shit Mari, you're so fucking tight!" I get myself seated halfway and pull almost all the way out, then back in getting deeper and deeper. She's making these moaning noises that are driving me crazy and I want to bang her brains out, but she needs me to be tender with her, she needs this. *She needs me!* I move from my hands to my elbows, then I grab her shoulders from underneath while placing my head in the crook of her neck. She instinctively wraps her legs around my waist. I pull her to me, sliding my shaft all the way in; she's becomes wetter and wetter with every stroke. I pick up the pace just a bit and she grabs my head to get me to look at her, and I notice a tear sliding down her face.

"Mari, you alright? Am I hurting you?"

"Mmmm I—I'm perfect, don't stop."

I lean in and kiss her, and she kisses me, ravenously, like she can't survive without it. The longer we kiss, the tighter her pussy clenches down on my shaft. Damn, I swear her pussy was made for me. I slam into her once and stroke a few times really, really slow. I can tell she *really* likes that. She's digging into my shoulders now. I slam into her again, stroking in and out slowly.

"You got some cum for me?"

"Mmmm, not yet Jordan, don't make me cum yet."

"I don't think you'll have a choice love." I slam into her again, but this time I'm changing positions because I'm not going to last much longer myself. I grab her legs and bring them both up toward her head. Jesus, we both writhe at the feel. I can't stop now, it feels too fuckin' good and the noises she makes are egging me on.

"Oh God, Jordan, don't stop, right there, don't stop, right there."

"Shit baby give me a squeeze!" And why the fuck did I say that. I let out a tsunami of cum deep inside her and at the same time she lets go, pulsing around my shaft, draining me dry. I collapse on top of her and when I try to move, her death grip holds me in place. I look at her and she is so goddamn beautiful. She grabs my face again to pull me in for a kiss but this time it's tender, like she missed me or something. "You okay baby?"

"More than okay." Now she releases me and I lie beside her, pulling her close, leaning my forehead against hers. She continues, "I think for the first time in my life I actually am okay. I know I'm going to sound crazy with what I'm about to say, but what do I need to do to get you to do this to me every single day for the rest of my life?"

"Was that a lonely girl proposal?"

"Do I even qualify anymore as being lonely? I think you might be stuck with me."

"You make it sound like 'being stuck with you' is a bad thing."

"Hmm, it might be."

"Somehow, I seriously doubt that but I look forward to finding out."

"Really?"

"Why is that surprising?"

"No reason."

"Okay . . . you're not ready to talk about it, I get it."

I get up, so I can take a shower and get ready for work but Mari keeps me from moving.

"Where're you going?"

"Going to take a shower so I can get ready for work." Mari's face takes on an entirely different look all of a sudden. "Are you pouting?"

"Am I? I didn't even realize I was making a face, but I do feel some type of way knowing I'm not going to be by your side all day. What did you do to me?"

"I didn't do anything. You just let me in."

"I'm not sure how I feel about that."

"I bet, considering I'm probably the first person you let get close to you."

"Stop doing that."

"Sorry. Look, you're feeling a bit vulnerable, I get that and leaving you alone to ponder over it probably has you feeling a bit uncomfortable. It'll be okay Mari. You letting me in I take very, very seriously. I won't take advantage of that. Trust me, okay."

"Okay. Will I see you tonight?"

"Of course, whatever you want. You have my number; you can call or text me whenever you want, texting would be better. I'll be pretty busy, but if you message me, I will respond."

"Are you leaving right now?"

"Right after my shower. Why, you wanna join me?"

"I thought you'd never ask!"

Chapter 9

Kamari

Jordan wasn't kidding when he said he would push my boundaries. I have never felt this way before. I feel extremely close to him and I have no idea why. Well, let me re-phrase. He did rub on my body for hours and who wouldn't like that, but the fact he wasn't gonna give me the "D" actually had me thinking. Then on top of that, I came so hard, *multiple times actually*, geez who wouldn't want to drink his Kool-Aid all the time. Fuck, he's turned me into one of those women who are clingy, whiny and want to be around their boyfriend every frickin' moment. I'm so deep in thought on my feelings I don't even hear Jordan talking to me. "Sorry, what was that?"

"I asked what were you thinking about. Freaking out about how you're feeling?"

"If I have to tell you to stop doing that one more time I think I'm gonna scream."

He just smiles at me and damn, I melt. *Shit!* I walk around to his side of the bed and kiss him.

"What was that for?"

"After that smile, I had no choice."

"Couldn't keep those lips off me huh? I'll take that."

"Like you have a choice, now get the shower going, I have plans for you." He doesn't even comment. He shoots me another gorgeous smile, goes straight to the bathroom, turns on the shower, and jumps in. I follow him, step in behind him and this time I get to ogle his beautifully chiseled body. What is it about a man dripping wet? I watch him shampoo his hair and I grab the shower gel and sponge and start on his back. I wash him all over,

28

down over his firm ass, and down his legs. I chuck the shower sponge because I really want to use my hands. After he rinses his hair, I turn him around to face me and I soap every inch of his front. Hmmm . . . I finally get to see his dick up close and personal; I'm licking my lips already. I soap up his dick until he starts making noises, then I grab the showerhead to rinse him off. I move him to the back of the shower out of the water, so the water can hit my back, and I drop to my knees and swallow him whole. I can hear him groan as he grabs the shower door to steady himself and then the back of my head. A girl must be doing something right. I increase my suction and start massaging his balls.

"Shit Mari, you trying to suck the color off it?"

I run my tongue in between the opening of the tip and it drives him wild. At this point, I increase my speed and he lets go of my head to brace himself with both hands on the wall and shower door right before exploding. He almost loses his balance. I give him a second to catch his breath, so I stand up and start soaping my own body. When I turn around to rinse my back he grabs me, pulls me to him for a kiss and I feel it everywhere. It's like butterflies in my stomach and electric pulses from my lips down to my toes. I have never actually felt anything for anyone one when kissing. I kiss mostly to keep the guy from talking. Some guys try to talk dirty but it's usually just an epic fail. Instead of telling them to shut up, I just cover their mouth with mine . . . everybody wins, well unless they can't kiss.

He runs his hands down my back slowly; oh my God I love his touch. He gives my ass a squeeze before lightly tracing his fingers over the crack of my ass to pull my legs apart as he picks me up. I wrap my legs around his waist as he pushes me against the wall. He slides his dick right in without using his hand, and we fit like two perfect puzzle pieces. He strokes me against the wall while never breaking the kiss and it's driving me insane. Then, he breaks the kiss to put one of my nipples in his mouth and my pussy clenches on his dick; we both groan. He palms my

29

ass so he can drive into me deeper and *shit* he feels so fuckin' good. He strokes me until he brings me to the brink, and he seems to know exactly when that is. He puts me down, turns me around, kicks my legs apart, and bends me over. As soon as my hands hit the wall, he's back inside me. .I can't take it. He is pounding me like nobody's business. Then all of a sudden, he slows his stroke and reaches around my waist to rub my clit. Why the fuck did he do that?! If I didn't lose my mind before, it's definitely oozing out of my ears now. He knows I can't handle a double assault and the noises I'm making sound like I'm in some sleazy porno. He starts pounding me again and rubbing my clit faster, the more he rubs my clit the more my pussy clenches on his dick; I have no control anymore. I'm pushing back into his hips but also grinding on his finger; it's like he's pushing an automatic button or something and I, I, oh my fuckin' God.

Chapter 10

JT

As soon as I started rubbing on Mari's clit I knew she wouldn't last long. She is so used to being in control. I have to show her it's okay if someone else takes the reins, but I had to knock down her walls in order for her to let me in. I let her have her way with me at first, but also took control back by tending to her needs. She thinks she wants to be fucked, but she's used to being with guys who don't actually care about her. There is something special about this one, as soon as I looked into her eyes I had to make her mine. Now that she is, she just has to come to terms that I belong to her. Her pussy and heart knows it but her head hasn't gotten the memo. She'll struggle with it for a while, but she'll come around.

We re-shower before exiting. I towel off, wrap the towel around my waist, and start drying Mari. She's giving me this 'I can take care of myself' look. I ask her, "What's wrong?"

"You know I can do that right?"

"Of course, but I want to make sure you miss me while I'm away. Baby oil or cocoa butter?"

"Cocoa butter. Wait, you want me to miss you?"

"Well, I'm a guy; I want you to think about me all the time."

"Considering what you've done to me in the last several hours, I don't think I'll have a choice."

We walk to the bed and I start applying the cocoa butter to her entire beautiful body. "I know you have some things to sort out, I just want to make sure I'm at the top of that list."

"Of course you are! *Shit*! Did I just say that out loud?"

31

"It's okay baby. We don't have to discuss this now. Like I said, you need some time to think. I'll be gone the majority of the day. How about dinner tonight?"

She takes the lotion from my hands when I get to her legs and says "Dinner sounds great. I'll finish up. If I keep letting you rub all over me, I'll never get out of this room and neither will you."

"Hmm, you need another hit? I don't punch a clock." I say wiggling my eyebrows.

"I know this is your room, but get out and let me get dressed!"

"How about I get dressed over in that corner so I can watch you finish, that way if you need me to jump back in, I'll be close by?"

"If you watch me, I don't think you'll be able to zip your pants."

"That depends on whether you'll be working with the lotion only? I mean this is supposed to be just a lotioning session after a shower, but if you're gonna go off script, why should I even get dressed?"

"You're right."

She gets up, grabs her clothes and goes into the bathroom. I even hear the click of the lock. I go to the door to listen and I can hear her panting on the other side and talking to herself . . ."*Oh God that was a close one. I just want to fuck him all the time now. What is wrong with me?!*" I step away from the door, smiling to myself, to get dressed, but I wait for her to come out before I leave.

"You alright?"

"Yeah, I'm good."

"Good. I'm going. Dinner tonight around 7?"

"Sounds like a plan."

     I walk over to her and pull her in for a kiss. She seems to melt into my arms and her breathing changes. Whatever she's feeling, I'm feeling it too. I start to kiss her down her neck as she caresses my back. I grunt a little because she feels so good and I don't want to stop, but now I understand where she's coming from. If we keep going like this, I'll never get out of here. I rest my head in the crook of her neck and she breathes a sigh of relief. I look her in the eyes before giving her another kiss. I back away. "Hey make sure you wear comfortable shoes tonight. The restaurant is close by and the weather is nice; I want to enjoy it before that sandstorm hits."

"Ok, I'll go by my room and change. I need to go for a run"

"What I wouldn't give to see that outfit."

"Well you can come back early and help me shower. OH MY GOD, we're doing it again. GO TO WORK!!"

     I laugh, kiss her on the forehead, give her a tap on the ass, and leave.

Chapter 11

Kamari

I finally leave Jordan's room and go back to mine. I change into my running clothes, grab a banana from the buffet as they were cleaning up, and hit the pavement. I decide to keep it simple and run around a 3-block radius so I can concentrate on whatever the hell is happening between me and Jordan and not my running route. I can't be falling for him already, I just met the man. I never have feelings for anyone. How did he break me down and get inside my head so quickly? Just thinking about him makes me wet, is this a lust thing? No, it's more than that. It's like he's everything I would ever want in a man but that's not something I've really thought about having, and considering my line of work, I can't get close. I have to put a stop to this. I'm crazy if I think I'm in any position to have an actual relationship with him. Shit, this is insane! He's not pressuring me for anything. He's not obsessing over me. He put his number in my phone giving me the power to call or not. He's the complete opposite of every man I have ever come across. He's right, he's not like most guys and I find myself not ever wanting to leave his side. Oh my God, what the fuck is wrong with me?

I return to my room dripping wet. I ran longer than expected and now I have about 2 hours before Jordan returns to take me to dinner. I peel out of my clothes and hop in the shower no closer to making a decision or sorting my feelings. This shower is not helping, as all I can think about now is our shower session from this morning. I can feel his touch all over me, making me feel so good, shit, making me feel . . . period. He makes me feel like I need him, but what will happen when he knows everything about me, will he bail? The thought of losing him almost brings me to tears. If that ain't some sick, twisted shit. Me, crying over a guy. I need to turn in my assassin's card right the fuck now. Jesus!

I decided to text Jordan, I didn't want to bother him while he was at work. Thank God I had some kind of restraint, but I did want him to know that I thought about him the entire day, ya know, stroke his ego a wee bit not that he needed it. He knows what I'm thinking before I do. Maybe he can help me process what I'm going through.

Me: Hey Jordan, ur plan worked; thought about u all day
Jordan: You've been on my mind all day 2. Missed u
Me: Really? <3, I've missed u 2; about 2nite, can we stay in?
Jordan: Sure, I can pick up sum food on the way back, get enough 4 a couple of days 2 ride out the storm
Me: Gr8, I'd rather just have u all 2 myself, plus I need 2 talk 2 u about sum things
Jordan: Ok, on my way. Any special requests food-wise?
Me: I have a feeling u know just what 2 get me
Jordan: U ok?
Me: Yeah, but I'll b better once u get here, so hurry up!
Jordan: Pedal 2 medal!!

I can't believe I just said everything I did in those texts to Jordan. I guess my body is just doing whatever the hell it wants and my body wants Jordan.

Chapter 12

JT

I pick up food for the both of us to last a few days, some bottled water, found some Sake, but not feeling the sushi around here since we're nowhere near an ocean, but this restaurant has baked salmon, lemon pepper and teriyaki, so I get both. I also get some sandwiches on wheat and rye bread, salad and fresh fruit, some ice and one of those stupid Styrofoam coolers for all the drinks. That should hold us for a bit. Maybe I can convince her to go out for ice cream later as we're going to be cooped up for a minute, better take advantage of getting out and about while we can.

I get back to the hotel and she meets me at the car. "Thought you could use a hand."

"Thanks. You take the food; I'll get the bottled water, ice, and cooler."

"Geez, you think you got enough?"

"Well, I wanted you to have a little bit of a choice."

"I don't see any beer. . ."

"The Sake will be enough." She has a big smile on her face.

"Any sushi?"

"No unfortunately. That restaurant I got the sushi from before ships it in fresh every other day and they closed a couple of days early for the storm. I didn't feel comfortable getting it from anywhere else, but I did get you two kinds of baked salmon."

"Good man!"

"I aim to please."

There's a bit of a buzz going around the hotel as they prepare for the storm. They are placing a special kind of filter over the "swamp coolers" to keep the sand out as the storm passes through. Swamp coolers are like air conditioners but they run with water to keep the humidity at an even level inside the building, keep pictures and wall paper from disintegrating since the air is so dry compared to the East Coast. I dump the ice in the cooler, while Mari puts whatever we're not eating in the mini fridge. Whatever doesn't fit goes in the cooler. Mari is looking out the window now. I can tell she's deep in thought. I walk up behind her and put my arms around her. She sinks into my touch, then she turns around for a real hug. "You alright?" I ask.

"Yeah, just enjoying the feel of you. You've become my favorite spot in the whole wide world."

I walk over to the bed and sit on it with my back against the headboard. I tap my lap, and tell her "come here." She walks over, straddles me and lies on my chest with her head in the crook of my neck. She begins to shake. "Mari, what's wrong? Hey, talk to me." I grab her face to look at her and her eyes are glassed over with unshed tears.

"I want to talk to you but I don't know how to begin. I'm afraid if I tell you anything about me, you won't want to stick around."

I kiss her forehead. "Come on baby, it can't be that bad." I look into her eyes, and they're telling me it's quite bad. She looks up to the ceiling, takes a deep breath, places the heel of her palms against both eyes to regain her composure. I remove her hands so I can see her face. "Ok, ok, calm down. Tell me what you feel comfortable sharing with me and we'll worry about the rest later. I'm not going anywhere, okay?"

"What is happening between us Jordan? I feel like . . . well hell, I don't even know how to describe it. You make me feel like I've known you the majority of my life or something, and I don't know how to process that. But the thought of not being with you is, is . . ."

"Scary?"

"Oh my God, YES!"

"So stop listening to your head. What's your heart telling you?"

"Well for some reason you seem to know me, like what I'm thinking and feeling, and knowing that is also scary but I feel you really wouldn't take advantage of that. So I feel that you would never hurt me and you actually want to take care of me, like I can trust you completely."

"Is that a bad thing?"

"I don't know how to do this, ya know, how to be in a relationship. I've never done that before."

"You've never had a boyfriend, even in high school?"

"No. When my parents died, I was angry with the world, to the point of hanging around with the wrong crowd, getting into fights, stealing. I trusted no one; so no, never been in a relationship."

"Okay, I get that. Do you feel safe with me?"

"Of course."

"And if I told you, you're mine and no one else's, how does that make you feel?"

"Safe and coveted, and knowing you can feel comfortable enough to tell me that soothes me. I feel the exact same way about you but not completely understanding why. I like knowing you want me all to yourself."

"Tell you what, let's eat. I know you want to stay in but let's go out for dessert because once the storm hits we'll be stuck in here for a while; you'll wish you got out of here while you had the chance."

"Okay."

"Is there something else you want to talk about?"

"Yeah but not tonight. Are you okay with that?"

"I know you'll tell me everything in due time. I'm not going to push. Okay?"

"What planet are you from? I've definitely hit the lottery with you Mr. Thompson."

"You bet your ass, future Mrs. Thompson."

"Stop that, because I actually like the sound of that."

***

After dinner, Mari and I go for a walk to the ice cream shop several blocks from the hotel. We sit and share a banana split with chocolate ice cream, her favorite, strawberry ice cream, my favorite, and in the middle is both our absolute favorite, blackberry. We talk about a lot of stuff, nothing serious, movies, music and surprisingly enough video games. We talked so much, the employees are looking at us funny because they need to close up and we're stopping them from doing that. So, we start walking back. Halfway back, I notice someone following us, Mari is talking about something but I'm not paying attention. I wrap my arm around her waist to pull her closer to me, as I notice another person from across the street walking toward us, *shit I think they're working to box us in*, which means someone is going to be in front of us any minute. I don't have my side arm, just my backup at my ankle (note to self, on duty or not, carry your fucking gun!). The three perps stop us, and the only thing I notice is Mari is not even scared.

"Look what we have here; it's the cutest couple in the world."

"Come on man, do you really want to do this?"

"I'm not doing anything . . . yet."

At that moment, the guy behind us pulls out a switchblade, and the first guy doing all the talking says, "Now give us your wallet and we'll be on our way." When the guy with the knife goes to grab Mari, I drop to one knee to grab my gun but the carnage going on around me stops me in my tracks. If I didn't watch it with my own eyes I wouldn't believe it, and I'm still having a hard time processing it even though it's unfolding before me.

Chapter 13

Kamari

I made these three guys the moment we left the ice cream shop. I think Jordan noticed them halfway back as he pulled me closer to him anticipating what was about to happen. When the guy behind us grabbed my shoulder, I dropped low and kicked his knee backwards; yeah, it's not supposed to bend like that! Jordan was down low, so I cartwheeled over him to drop kick the guy to his left, leaving Mr. Mouth looking at me scared shitless. I did a roundhouse to his head and he was out like a light. When I looked back at Jordan, let's just say he had a look on his face of shock and awe.

"What the fuck was that?!"

"Self-defense class, a girl's gotta protect herself." He grabs my hand and we start walking back to the hotel faster than necessary.

"Mari, *that* was not self-defense; that was some Bruce Lee shit. Where did you learn to fight like that?"

"I told you I got into a lot of fights when I was younger."

"Yeah, but this is not something you pick up off the street either. Mari, I know you're not ready to tell me everything but don't lie to me."

"Okay, sorry. Not self-defense."

"Yeah, no shit." We get back to the hotel and I can't tell if he's mad at me or not and it's freaking me out because he's pacing back and forth.

"Are you mad at me?"

"What?! No, of course not. My adrenaline is pumping over the fact of what could've happened to us, to you. Just give me a few minutes, it'll pass. While I try to calm down, just tell me about your training, and I promise I won't ask any more questions tonight."

"Well, when my parents died, I didn't want to end up in an orphanage as my father was an only child and so was my mother. My father was military, so he taught me how to fight some but once I was on the streets of Japan, that didn't get me far. I remember this kid beating me to a pulp and I promised myself I would never let that happen again. I walked into this Dojo and asked Sensei to teach me how to fight. He took me under his wing because he had a daughter my age who died recently due to some type of illness. I know almost all forms of martial arts including weaponry. You can ask whatever you want, but I get to say whether I feel comfortable telling you. I have never, *ever* told anyone, and I mean anyone, what I just told you."

I can see Jordan is beginning to calm, but surprisingly he is not saying anything and that scares me.

"Wow, you're a badass huh?"

"Really? After everything I just said, that's your first question?" He pulls me in for a hug that I didn't know I needed until he wrapped his arms around me.

"Come here. First, I want to thank you because I know it was hard for you to share that with me. Second, I'm just glad they didn't hurt you, not that they could but let me look you over, you may not realize you have any wounds as I'm sure adrenaline is running through your veins as well."

"I'm alright Jordan."

"Mari, the thought of someone hurting you fucked my head up. Considering your training, I know I don't have to worry about you per sé, but it doesn't mean I won't worry. Okay?"

"Okay."

"Shit, you have no idea how bad I want to fuck you right now?"

I start pulling my clothes off and he starts doing the same; we can't get them off fast enough. We made love all night, I never even heard the storm when it passed by.

Chapter 14

I wake up early the next morning after making love to Mari all night. She has me in her death grip again and I love it. My mind is racing though, going over everything she said to me about her fighting background and then it dawns on me. What a fucking coincidence this has to be. The murders by pressure points, the murders by Japanese plant poison, and now I practically find the love of my life who's from Japan with martial art skills out the ass. I don't believe in coincidences.

Mari starts to stir and she goes straight for my dick. We make love again; shit, I can't get enough of her; she's like a drug. Over the next two days after the storm, we talk, eat, sleep and fuck waiting for the area to get cleaned up so we can go out, not that we're tired of being cooped up but we can stand to have some fresh air. By day three, we go out to eat. I have Mari grab us a table while I check in with the station. I want to let my guy in NY know I sent him a hair sample and give him the case number to the unknown DNA Jeremy logged into the Federal system. He'll handle it to where it will be undetected with results sent to me as I need to know what I'm dealing with before I make my next move.

We decided to go to the restaurant closest to the airport. It's the best place to be as they're directly connected to the airport, so anyone flying out can go through security and wait for their flight over here. The place is packed. They have a ridiculous amount of TVs with several dedicated to incoming and outgoing flights. So we'll know when flights are going west before anyone else. I'm drinking a beer—finally—and we're sharing a veggie pizza when Mari goes to the restroom. Out of the blue, this guy who looks familiar walks up to me and asks,

"What are you doing here with her?"

"Excuse me?"

"What are you doing here with Mar; it doesn't seem like official police business."

"Hmm, I remember you. You're Mack. I spoke to you about the death of one of your coworkers."

"Yeah that's me. What are you doing with her? She's mine!"

At this point, I decide to stand because the stupidness coming out of his mouth is not going to get me sucker punched in a seated position. "She doesn't belong to anyone, and if she belonged to you, and that's a big if, don't you think she would've told me?" I didn't want to provoke him by telling him she's mine, but by the look in his eyes, this is not going to end well, just not sure for whom just yet.

"YOU CAN'T HAVE HER!!" And this muthafucka pulls out a gun. The crowd goes nuts, running out and ducking under tables. Here we go with another incident where a black guy pulls a gun on another black guy in a mostly white establishment. Yeah, this will be on the news later.

"Look Mack, this is not something you want to be doing. Look around you, you're scarring the patrons and I know you don't want to go to jail for killing a cop right?"

He laughs, maniacally, and says, "I don't give a fuck who you are, you can't have her!!" And then I hear three pops, more screams and I start fading in and out of consciousness.

Chapter 15

Kamari

      I go to the bathroom because clearly I drank too much, and by the time I wash my hands I hear gunshots and my heart sinks. I run out to see what is going on and I see a large amount of people around my table. When I push my way through, OH MY GOD, it's Jordan. He's been shot, and there's blood everywhere.

"Oh my God Jordan, what happened? Who did this to you?" I shout to the crowd, "Did someone call 911?" Someone responded that an ambulance was on the way. Jordan grabs my hand.

"Mari, grab my phone." He's gasping for air, as he was shot in the chest twice and a third bullet grazed his head. "Call Hank [wheeze], tell him what happened [gasp], where we are [cough], and what hospital I'm going to [wheeze]. He'll handle the rest."

Tears are streaming down my face now, I can barely see through them. "Jordan, who did this?"

"No Mari, [wheeze] promise me [cough] you won't [wheeze] take matters [cough] into your own hands!"

"But Jordan, you have to tell me so I can take care of it?" He starts choking, and oh my God it sounds like he's dying and I can't imagine my life without him. "Jordan, don't you fuckin' die on me! You hear me!? I just found you, don't leave me alone in this world again!"

"Mari, promise me . . ."

"I promise."

      He reaches up to touch my cheek and I place my hand over his, then kiss the inside of his hand when he says, "I love you." His hand goes limp and he stops talking, did he stop breathing? Oh God! The paramedics move me out of the way to work on him. When I see and hear the heart monitor showing a heartbeat I breathe a sigh of relief and I use Jordan's phone to call Hank.

"JT, bruh, glad to hear you made it through the storm. When you coming back?"

"Hank, this is Kamari. Jordan's been shot."

"What? Shot?! What the fuck happened, and who the hell are you?"

"Shut up and listen! Paramedics are working on him now; they'll be taking him to Grand Canyon Memorial. I wasn't with him when the shooting happened but he knows who did it. He said if I called you, you'd take care of everything. I don't know what that means and I don't care. I'll be at the hospital when you get there. Do I need to repeat anything?"

"No, I got it. I'll make a few calls. I'm not sure how soon I can get there as flights from the west are still a no-go. I'll make you point person until I get there. If JT trusts you to call me, I'll follow his lead, but only until I get there. Understand?"

"Understood."

"Hey, make sure you text me with updates. I don't wanna be bouncing off the walls worrying. I'll text you when I get a flight out there."

"Okay."

* * *

I get to the hospital and Jordan is still in surgery. I'm pacing around the waiting room seething, wanting to go after whoever did this when it hits me. I know exactly who did this; it's fuckin' Mack. SHIT! I knew he was obsessing but I didn't think he'd go this far. I swear to God I will kill him with my fuckin' bare hands but not until I know Jordan's gonna be okay. The doctor comes out and walks straight to me. I've never been so nervous before in my life.

"Mrs. Thompson?"

Why do I love the way that sounds? "Yes."

"Your husband did great! He's a strong one. He lost a lot of blood. He took a bullet to one lung and one to the shoulder, but both passed right through actually. The one to his head was just a graze. He won't even need stitches for that one."

"Thank God! Can I see him?"

"Sure, they're taking him up to his room now. He's pretty heavily sedated for the pain, so he'll be out for at least a day or two, maybe longer considering the amount of blood he lost. I'll walk you up in case you have any questions for me."

"I do actually, do you think I can move him to another hospital. We were waiting for the storm to pass so we can go back west. I know he'd rather heal at home."

"Sure, we need to keep him a day or two to ensure he's stable, then you should be able to move him. Just make sure you have a nurse to check his wounds and change the bandages once a day, don't want them getting infected."

We get to the end of the hall and I notice there are two cops, one standing on each side of the door. I ask the doctor, "What's with the protection?"

"Well I'm sure being the wife of a cop I don't have to tell you that's standard procedure. Don't want whoever shot him coming back and finishing the job; you'd have to be crazy to shoot a cop."

"Right. Thanks doc, I appreciate the information." I walk into Jordan's room and he looks like he's been through the wringer. I grab his hand and whisper in his ear. "Hey baby, I'm here and I'm not going anywhere until you wake up." I kiss his forehead and he squeezes my hand. I pull the chair next to the bed with my foot as Jordan won't let my hand go and I place my head against the bed right next to our hands, so I know when he stirs. I'm not leaving this room until I know he's safe. I dropped the ball in that restaurant; it won't happen again.

***

The next day, Jordan's phone goes off in my pocket; it's Hank telling me he just landed and making his way to the hospital; I text him the room number. Twenty minutes later I hear a knock at the door. A guy sticks his head in and says, "Kamari? It's Hank."

"Come in Hank."

"How's he doing?"

"He's good. Came through surgery just fine, but he's been completely out of it since surgery, lost a lot of blood as both bullets passed right through. Third one grazed his head."

"Looks like whoever shot him tried to go for a head shot but missed as JT was falling."

I give Hank an evil look.

"Sorry. Did he tell you who did this?"

"No."

"Has he been awake at all?"

"No, he just squeezes my hand depending on what I say to him. Grab the other one and let him know you're here?"

"You think he'll hear me?"

"Yes."

Hank walks from the foot of the bed to the opposite side from where I'm already sitting and grabs Jordan's hand. I can tell he's really affected by what happened to him. He leans over and says, "Bruh, I can't leave you alone for a minute. You're gone for not even a week and now you're in the hospital. And you definitely haven't mentioned this beautiful queen by your bedside to me. You got some 'splaining to do' when you wake up and yes, I'm going to give you shit about it!" I can see Jordan squeezing his hand, several times. Hank looks at me like he wants to ask me something.

"What?"

"Who are you to JT?"

"Someone who cares about him? And who are you to Jordan, Hank?"

"I'm his brother, partner, and friend. Do you know who did this?"

I thought about telling Hank, but I'm not going to say anything until I can talk to Jordan. I can't blame him for not telling me he's a cop; it's not like I've been forthcoming with who I am. He probably already knows who I am, which makes me love him even more that he didn't bolt. I guess he was waiting for me to open up to him so he can do the same. Well hell, the cat's out of the bag now. I've got to get him out of here. He's not safe with Mack running around, he could've been following us and I didn't even notice. That's not like me. My thoughts are nothing but Jordan. I guess after the night we got mugged (or tried to be), I let my guard down and totally missed being watched by Mack. I finally answer Hank, "No, I don't know who did this. I asked Jordan but he fell unconscious before he could tell me."

"You look like you need some rest. Why don't you go and get some sleep?"

"No, I want to be here when Jordan wakes."

"I promise to call you as soon as he wakes up."

"Hank, I'm not leaving!"

"Okay, but you still look like you need a break, go get some coffee or something. Have you eaten?"

"Not since it happened?"

"Jesus woman, that was 24 hours ago!"

"Okay, okay, I'll go grab a coffee."

I walk down to the cafeteria when someone grabs me to pull me into a storage closest. Oh my God, it's fuckin' Mack. "Is he dead Mar?"

"Are you shittin' me? Why the fuck did you do this?"

"I had to Mar, you belong to me!"

The rage I'm feeling right now has surpassed anything I've ever felt before. "Mack, I'm going to say this to you one time. I love that man you tried to kill yesterday and it's taking every fiber of my being not to kill you where you fuckin' stand because I promised him I wouldn't take matters into my own hands. I want you to pack a bag and I don't give a fuck where you go but I promise you the next time you see me, I will be the last thing you ever see."

"You don't mean that."

I take two fingers and press them into his stomach just below the ribcage on a 45-degree angle, like I'm actually trying to grab his rib bone; it inflicts a ridiculous amount of pain and keeps the person from moving. I grab rags off the shelf and stuff them into his mouth, then cover it with my other hand so no one hears the screams coming from this closet. I speak to him extremely calm with a side of menacing in my voice. "Do you feel that?" He nods his head while squirming in pain. "In your mind, I want you to think how this would feel if you multiply it by 10 or even 100, since most men can't handle real pain. That does not even begin to describe what I will do to you if you harm another hair on that man's head! Do you understand me?" He nods his head again. "I suggest you leave and pray the cops find you before I do, as I will not be responsible for the fury I will unleash upon you. You will be targeted as someone who tried to kill a cop, and that is actually a safer alternative for you compared to what I will do to you. I never want to hear from you again. Do you understand me?!" He nods fearfully and I walk out. I grab my coffee, some fruit and go back to Jordan's room. "How's the patient?"

"He's fine, didn't move at all. What happened to you; I thought you got lost for a second?"

"No, I went to splash some water on my face. Brought you a coffee. You look like a regular Joe kinda guy with cream and sugar."

"Yeah, that's right. Wow, you're like a female version of JT. I get it."

Before I came back to the room, I made a few calls, now that all the flights are back to normal. I made arrangements to have Jordan moved to my penthouse in Seattle. I can't take any chances with Mack walking the very halls of this hospital. I don't know if I got through to him and I'm not waiting to find out. Later that night, Hank leaves to check into a hotel, as he was trying to wait for rooms to become available as people can finally fly out west. I tell the cops at the door they can both take a break and my people moved in with the quickness. I charted a private jet to move Jordan, signed all the discharge papers and hired a private ambulance to take him to the airstrip. I packed both our rooms at the hotel and checked out. I even had the rental car company go and pick up his rental when I turned mine in. There will be no trace of us here other than his hospital records and I paid that bill as well. I remove the battery from Jordan's phone so it can't be traced. We're ghost!

Chapter 16

I wake slowly in a lot of pain in unfamiliar surroundings. The bandages around my torso are pretty tight, keeping me from breathing deeply. My left arm is pinned to my bandages to keep it immobile. I keep looking around the room and the only thing I recognize is Mari nuzzled on my right side with her head on my shoulder. Her arms are crossed in front of her with the fingers of her left hand intertwined with my right. I guess her arms are crossed to keep from crushing my injuries in her death grip I love so much. I pick my head up slowly to kiss her on the forehead, which wakes her and then she asks,

"Hey baby, how're you feeling?"

"I've been better. Where are we?"

"My place."

"And where is that exactly?"

"Does it matter?"

"At this moment, not really. I'm just naturally inquisitive."

She leaves my side to grab a bottle of water on the nightstand, cracks it open and puts a bendy straw inside.

"Here, drink some water. I know your throat is dry."

She's right, as I drink like I've been walking the desert for a month.

"Hey slow down . . . small sips . . . good. You hungry?"

"Starved. How long have I been out?"

54

"Four days."

"You're fuckin' kidding me! That bastard got me good huh?"

"Don't even joke about that. I made some miso soup and some chicken noodle. Doc said with all the drugs and not eating solid food to start you off slowly. The chicken noodle may be too heavy, so I did the miso just in case."

"The miso sounds great."

Mari comes back with a tray of soup and some buttered bread with a glass of OJ. I try to sit up, but it's not working. When I try again, Mari has already put the tray down on the other side of the bed to stack pillows behind my back so I can sit up comfortably. Just moving fuckin' hurts as I strain myself moving around, which makes me breathe harder, which I can't fuckin' do because of the damn bandages. She places the tray in front of me, puts a cloth napkin around my neck and actually starts feeding me. I give her a weird look.

"Don't look at me like that. It's no different than when you wanted to lotion my body the other day. Plus, you're in a lot of pain, the less you move the better including feeding yourself. How's your pain level?"

"It's a bitch."

"The docs had you pretty heavily sedated. Your drugs were through IV and those ended yesterday, which is probably why you woke up today. I'll give you your medicine after you eat, don't want you taking them on an empty stomach. The medicine has antibiotics in them too to stave off wound infection."

"So while I sit here being fed, mind bringing me up to speed?"

"Sure. Where you want me to start?"

"Start when I blacked out on you and take me through how we ended up here."

"Well, when you blacked out, the paramedics had arrived so I did what you asked and called Hank. I told him everything you told me to tell him. When I got to the hospital, you were still in surgery and I was a fuckin' wreck by the way. Hank got there the next day as the flights from the west coast opened back up."

"I remember hearing him talk shit to me."

"Is that all you remember?"

"I heard you too babe, you never let go of my hand; if you did, it wasn't for long. The drugs had me not completely out but I can tell the difference. With those drugs, it had my breathing slower and shallower, so less painful. Now, I just hurt with every breath."

"I left your side because Hank begged me to get something to eat. It was about 24 hours since I had anything. So I went to the cafeteria to grab something when someone pulled me into a storage closet."

"I guess I don't have to ask who that was. What did you do?"

"I promised you I wouldn't do anything, but I gave him a warning to drop off the face of the fuckin' planet before I get a hold of him or he'll be sorry."

"Mari, that guy is pretty big. You threatened him?" She gave me a look, and then I remembered who I was actually talking to. "What did you tell him exactly?"

"I put two fingers together and drove them at a 45-degree angle between his stomach and ribcage so I could actually grab his rib. It's a pretty excruciatingly painful move. I had to cover his mouth to keep his screams from being heard."

"Jesus Mari!"

"I told him it was taking every ounce of self-control to keep from killing him where he stood but I promised you I wouldn't take matters into my own hands and if he harmed one hair on your head, he should pray the cops find him first because if I got a hold of him, I would be the last thing he saw."

"Remind me not to get on your bad side."

"He had a lot of fear in his eyes, but that might have been the craziness. I told him that I loved you and I never wanted to see him again, as I would not be responsible for my actions. I'm not sure if I got through to him Jordan, so I made arrangements to have you moved here."

I finish with the soup Mari was giving me and started sipping on the juice while she continued to update me.

"I checked us out of the hotel, packed up everything, turned in the car rentals, paid your hospital bill, booked a private ambulance, and charted a private jet to have you moved after you were stable. That was two days after the incident. Your side arm, back up and shield are on the dresser. Your phone is to your left on the nightstand but I removed the battery so we wouldn't be tracked as I can't figure out how Mack found us."

"Well Mari, I have to say your skills for going ghost are epic. Did you remove the SIM card?"

"No, I was going to destroy it, but I wasn't sure if you had information on there you needed access to."

"Do me a favor, grab my small duffle; the side pocket has some SIM cards in there. Grab me one from the blue side."

"What are these?" She says while handing me one of the cards.

"They're buried SIMs, gives me a way to use my phone without it being traced. It's still linked to my old number, so if you call me, it'll come through but my regular number is buried under a second number. When I call from this number, it'll show but when you call that specific number, you won't get anything as the number is registered as not in service."

"Wow, that's brilliant. You gonna take your medicine?"

"Not yet, I need to get Hank on Mack and check in with my aunt. I'm sure she's probably heard by now and I don't want her to worry."

"Oh my God, Jordan, I didn't even think about your family. They must be worried sick."

"It's okay babe. You did everything right. Without knowing what Mack was going to pull, I appreciate you taking care of me, really."

When I changed the SIM, replaced the battery and turned the phone on, the phone goes nuts with messages out the wahzoo. I call Hank first.

"This is Walters."

"Hank, it's JT."

"Fuck JT, where the hell are you!? I came back to the hospital the next day and you and little girlfriend were gone. Doc said *your wife* checked you out and went home and of course I had no idea where that was. Who the hell is that chick?"

"Hank! Focus! Call Lieu in Reno to put out an APB for Andre Mack. I doubt he left from Arizona and went back home but start there."

"Ok man, but you gotta tell me something; we're all worried about you JT. I'm really nervous about this shit. What's going on?"

"Mari saw Mack at the hospital. She felt you wouldn't be able to protect me, so she ghosted us."

"Shit man, who is this super chick and does she have a sister?"

"No, she does not have a sister. I've missed you man. Look, I need time to heal before I can do anything. Mari's got me okay. I'll be down for at least 3-4 weeks. You can still reach me at the same number, you just can't track me. I don't know what Mack is capable of, so I need the people closest to me to be safe and that includes you alright."

"Ok JT, I'm on it. I'll text you with any updates."

"And I'll do the same." [End call].

"Babe, can you get me another bowl of that soup?"

"Sure love."

While Mari is in the other room, I look for a message from my contact in NY. He texted only one word . . . 'match.' I already knew that before I sent it, I just needed confirmation. I call my Aunt Reyna. "Hello?"

"Hey Aunt Rey-Rey, it's JT."

"Oh my God baby where are you? You've been all over the news and your phone has been rolling to voice mail. Are you okay?"

"Yes ma'am. Sorry about that." Mari returns with the soup, but places it on the dresser so she can sit next to me on the bed. "I had to be placed in protective custody. So my phone was off limits for a bit."

"I'm glad you're alright. Who's the girl?"

"What? What girl?" I squeeze Mari's hand.

"You sound like you found someone special."

"Come on Auntie, there is no way you can tell by my voice that I met someone." At this point, Mari is giggling into my shoulder.

"JT?"

"Yes, I've met someone. She's practically my bodyguard. You'll meet her over the holidays okay? Love you too!"

Chapter 17

Kamari

The one-sided conversation I heard Jordan having with his aunt was adorable. How I miss having family. I felt loved when he told her I would meet her over the holidays. At least I know he's not getting rid of me just yet. Jordan hangs up from his aunt and looks at me with concern.

"Ok Mari, now for the elephant in the room. You need to tell me everything, and I mean absolutely everything. The situation we are in now requires it."

"You promise whatever I tell you, you won't bail?"

"What, are you kidding? Don't you think if I were going to bail it would have happened before now? I love you Mari and I will do absolutely anything in my power to keep you safe. Now spill."

I tell Jordan everything, from the time my Sensei trained me, created the poison for me, to the attack in the alley, to being an assassin for hire. Then he starts asking questions.

"How do you know Mack?"

"Actually, he was my original target but with a stipulation."

"Stipulation?"

"Yeah, it's when the target isn't actually confirmed yet or a definite. So a second message will come through later confirming the target or changing who the target originally was. It's the client's way of blocking your availability until confirmed. Mack was the original target, but it changed to Dwight Freeman."

"So what happened after the target changed?"

"I figured Mack was a good looking guy and I could use him to take care of my own needs."

"And he's been wanting to drink that Kool-Aid ever since . . ."

"Well, he was more tolerable than most, so I made the mistake of inviting him on a trip to my cabin in the mountains. I took some downtime and didn't want to go alone. He came up for a week; he wanted more like they all do, but like the rest I shut him down. I had rules in place, ya know, ask no questions, this isn't serious, don't expect something to come out of it, yadda, yadda, yadda."

"But he thought he could change your mind."

"Yeah. I was even considering giving him a 'standing appointment' just to get my rocks off when I needed, but Hurricane Jordan hit me out of nowhere." Jordan winks at me, which makes me feel tingles down to my clit. "Tell me something Jordan. Although Mack is taking it to the extreme, why do all these guys become so obsessive with me? I don't get it."

"Well considering I've had a taste of the Kool-Aid, I actually get it. That first night I met you, when I looked into your eyes I had to make you mine, but I had let you call the shots. I mean women have all the power right? Once I knocked down your walls and you let me in, I couldn't get out if I wanted to and trust me, I didn't want to. I had to let you figure things out on your own. The hardest thing I had to do was wait for that. You are all I think about when I'm with you or not. I guess it's sort of like our souls meshing. You were in a dark place before me, which is why you never opened up to anyone. When you were with a guy, maybe that darkness corrupted them somehow making them obsessive. With Mack, he was with you more than once, so his 'corruption' was more profound driving him over the edge."

"That sounds kinda ridiculous."

"Yeah, maybe it's the pain talking. Where're those pills?"

"Here you go baby." After Jordan, takes the pills, I remove most of the pillows so he can lie back.

"First let me come to terms that you are actually a live, breathing assassin . . . I mean, that's not something you come across every day. I thought assassins were extinct or something. You really are a badass. You're not afraid of anything in your line of work huh?"

"Not until recently."

"Really, what are you afraid of now?"

"Losing you!"

"Not gonna happen, babe. I'm not going anywhere, promise. Come here baby, lay with me. I'll come up with a plan to fix all this but you've got to trust me okay."

"Okay, but this is not an easy fix."

"It'll be okay," Jordan is talking a lot slower now like he's falling asleep, "but I'm in too much pain to think stra—." The pills knock Jordan out. He'll have to be a magician to get me out of this shit storm.

Chapter 18

JT

I wake up but this time I find that I'm in bed alone. I hear thumping, not sure what it is, so I decide to get up. It still hurts to move, but I've been in bed long enough. Plus, I haven't been on my legs until they took me off the IV medications. As I walk through the living room, I'm noticing how huge this place really is; seems like the longer I walk the longer it gets. Geez, it's a frickin' penthouse. I follow the sound to a room where Mari is kicking the shit out of a punching bag. She's wearing earplugs, so she doesn't notice me yet. I don't mind watching her in action; she's beautiful even covered in sweat. I'm amazed how high she can kick, like she can kick herself in her own head if she tried. She turns around and sees me staring at her. I never get tired of looking at her smile. She removes the earplugs, comes up to me to kiss me and says,

"Why are you up out of bed so early in the morning?"

"Hell, I don't even know what time it is."

"Umm, it's a little after 5 a.m."

"5 a.m.?! Shit, doesn't feel like it. Plus, I was out for four days straight; I think I'm all rested."

"The rest you need has nothing to do with sleep love. How much pain are you in?"

"It only hurts when I breathe hard."

"Which you're doing because you've walked across the entire penthouse. Come on, back to bed."

"I can sit here watch you work out. It's better than watching TV!"

64

"You could but then I couldn't concentrate with you watching me. I'm not used to having an audience."

"I can watch you shower."

"Absolutely not! You're nowhere in any kind of shape to do that. Don't start something we can't finish. Why do you think I'm kicking the shit out of the punching bag? It's taking everything in me to keep from ravaging you in your sleep!"

"You serious?!" She's looking at me like she is deadly serious. It's adorable.

"I went from having you every single day, sometimes 2 or 3 times a day, to being cut off cold turkey. I'm definitely in withdrawal." She winks at me. "Go back to bed or do you want breakfast?"

"Naw too early. I'll grab some juice on the way back, not sure if I'll be able to go back to sleep though."

"Give me 30 minutes. After all your shower talk, I need 30 more kicks to the bag before my shower."

"Yeah, now I'm thinking about it again. Actually, I wouldn't mind a shower myself. What time is the nurse coming? Maybe I can shower before she gets here, then she can apply fresh bandages."

"You realize you can't shower alone right?"

"I know that. Why do you think I'm running it by you? I just have to know you can control yourself."

"Let me get this straight. You want me to get in the shower with you, naked, and I'm only supposed to help you clean up? Someone is going to get hurt."

"Yeah, that does sound dangerous."

"I got it, I'll bathe you. We'll keep the water low so the water doesn't mess with your wounds."

"I guess turnabout is fair play huh? I'm down with that."

"I'll get the water ready, no bubbles. Nurse will be here at 7. We should be done if we start right now."

"Am I moving that slow?"

"Why yes, yes you are."

Chapter 19

Kamari

I get the bathroom ready. I change my mind again, I can't have him sitting in water, it's not like I can help him in the tub or get him out for that matter. I considered the shower again, but if he slips, that leaves me trying to help him up. What to do? What to do? Got it!! I pull everything together when Jordan slowly walks in. I tell him,

"Here, have a seat by the sink. I'm going to shave you first. The love of my life is under there somewhere."

"It's not that bad is it? Whoa, is that an actual straight razor!?"

"Yeah, it cuts cleaner than a razor blade or an electric one. Don't worry, I used to shave my dad all the time and he was in the military; so you know I'm good at it."

"Normally, I would agree with you but how long ago was that?"

"Come on, don't be such a girl." I help him sit and he's breathing a bit hard, so I give him a few minutes to catch his breath. "Don't worry, I promise you won't feel a thing."

"Ok, I guess I don't have a choice. I trust you but that might be the remaining drugs in my system." He winks at me.

Jordan finally begins to breathe normally. I tell him to lean his head back so I can put a hot towel on his face.

"Shit Mari, that's hot." He sounds muffled under the towel.

"The towel is supposed to be, silly. Just relax. I'm surprised you can feel it with all that facial hair."

"I still say you're exaggerating."

67

I remove the towel and apply the shaving cream, then begin shaving him. He's looking right into my eyes as I work. "What?"

"Nothing, can't a guy enjoy the view?"

I kiss him on the forehead and place a dollop of shaving cream on his nose. He really doesn't have that much hair on his face considering it's been almost a week since he shaved, but I love him clean shaven. "All done. See, I didn't even nick you once."

"I had no doubts."

"Yeah right! I'm going to place another hot towel on your face, so man up. After that, I'll hit you with the aftershave, which will be the true test on how well I did." While the towel sits on Jordan's face, I place an extra-thick, fluffy towel on the floor of the tub. I do not run any water. I walk back to him to remove the towel and pat his face with the aftershave. Then I ask, "Any burning?"

"Surprisingly no and that's a first."

I place my cheek against his, "How I've missed your face!" I pull out the gauze scissors left by the nurse. Jordan looks at me horrified and says,

"You're not cutting my hair with those!"

"Oh my God you're ridiculous. I'm going to cut off your bandages before putting you in the tub. I'll let you take care of your own hair. I think your facial hair grows faster than what's on your head." I finish cutting away the bandages. "Your wounds look pretty good. Let me help you into the tub."

"Ok, how are we working this?"

I walk with Jordan over to the tub. I remove his boxers. I tell him, "Sit on the edge and swing your legs inside. Use you good arm to kneel onto the towel, that's why the towel is folded there. You'll kneel here while I use the shower head to bathe you. So, no fall risk, because I won't be able to pick you up."

"Ya know, you're kinda brilliant."

"Hmm, that's not the first time I've heard that." I hand him a dry towel to cover his face. "Lean forward a bit for me, I want to wash your hair. Use the towel to keep the shampoo and water out of your eyes. Plus, I don't want the shampoo running over your wounds." I use the shower head to wet his hair and massage his scalp, then I rinse. "Do I need to rinse and repeat?"

"Really?"

I laugh, which is something I've been doing a lot with him, laughing and smiling. I can't get enough. "Just checking." I take the towel from him and start wetting the rest of his body. The tub is pretty big, so I decide to stand in the tub with him (still in my work out clothes). I start soaping up his back and it reminds me when I showered with him the first time, and considering the state of his dick, he's thinking the same exact thing. "Jordan, you're starting to breath heavier, you alright."

"Considering, I'm kneeling in front of you butt naked and you're rubbing all over my body, I'm a bit . . . overwhelmed."

"Yeah, I've been there. You want me to make the water colder?"

"Honestly, I don't think that's gonna help."

"Ok, how 'bout this? I'm feeling overwhelmed myself but clearly, we can't do anything about it. So I'm going to give you your own advice. Just sit here and enjoy it."

"Have you really just graduated to using my own words against me?"

"Well, you did say earlier that turnabout was fair play."

"Funny, you just did it again."

I rinse off Jordan's back and move to stand in front of him. He's sporting a full-blown hard on now. Dammit, what I wouldn't give to sit on that. "Since I removed the bandages, does breathing still hurt?" Jordan takes a deep breath.

"Only if I do that deep breath doctors usually ask for."

"Let's test it." He cocks an eyebrow at me. I soap up Jordan's entire front including his extremely large dick. He grabs the side of the tub to steady himself while locking his eyes on me.

"Mari, as good as this feels maybe we . . . should. . . damn that feels so fuckin' good. You know . . . I'm in no condition . . . to reciprocate . . . right?"

"Jordan, this is about taking care of you. I can wait until you're 100% or close to it."

I rinse him off and soap him up again, extra lather this time and go to work. It didn't take long; poor baby, he needed this. I have a punching bag to tie me over. I ask him, "Does it hurt to breathe now."

"I'll take that any day over those damn pills."

"I bet you'll sleep better tonight too." I rinse him off again, then carefully dry his torso, back and front, being sure not to irritate his wounds. He uses his good arm to sit again on the edge of the tub and I dry his legs. He swings his legs out of the tub and I dry his feet. "Baby oil or cocoa butter?"

"You're on a roll aren't you? Baby oil."

I oil his body lightly except the top half of his torso, as I want the nurse to have an oil-free space to work on. Right when I helped him into fresh boxers and back to bed the doorbell rings.

"Damn Mari, you timed that perfectly."

"I'll let the nurse in, then start your breakfast after my shower."

"You're just trying to keep me from watching you."

I wink at him, then turn and walk away to get the door.

***

After my shower, I make Jordan silver dollar blueberry pancakes with some Canadian bacon. I make myself some soft scrambled eggs with parmesan cheese over whole grain toast; we have some fresh fruit to share and orange juice. I speak to the nurse on the way out to make sure everything went okay and walk her to the door. Then, I carry the breakfast trays into the room. "The nurse told me she loosened your bandages a bit and you can go in a sling next week."

"Yeah, I can breathe like a normal person now and wow those pancakes smell amazing!! Can I have that?"

"Yes, the doctor took you off the dietary restrictions but told us not to go crazy, hence the baby cakes and no 'real' bacon or sausage just yet, so I browned you some Canadian bacon instead."

I sit Jordan's tray in front of him, place the second tray in front of his and straddle his legs so I can eat. I'd rather sit in front of him than beside him. He looks at my plate and says,

"Yours looks better than mine."

71

"Mine doesn't have any meat, so I know you're pulling my leg but you're welcome to taste it if that's what you're getting at." He takes a stab at my eggs.

"Yo, those eggs are bomb!"

"You want half? I'll give you half my eggs for one of your baby cakes."

"Deal!"

I watch Jordan eat; his appetite is picking up. "You need me to make you some more; your appetite is definitely improving."

"Naw I better not, as I'm definitely going back to sleep after this. After our shower session and all the moving around this morning, I'm pretty wiped. I can feel the pain kicking in. Plus, since I can't work out, I don't want to lie around with too much food on my stomach."

"Ok, I'll clean up and get your medication. Hey, have you spoken to Hank?"

"Actually, I haven't even turned my phone on. I like being cut off from the rest of the world. All I need is you babe."

"If there's one thing I've learned in my existence, it's easy to become cut off from the rest of the world permanently. You won't realize it until it's too late, but you have family and friends who care about you and they would miss you too, so call Hank. I'm sure he would want to hear from you."

"I'll call him tomorrow. I promise."

* * *

I've noticed Jordan has been having trouble sleeping the last couple of nights, especially now that he is on less medication as he heals. I'm often awakened by him moaning in his sleep and not in a good way. When I place my hand on him to let him know I'm here, he's cold and clammy. My touch seems to calm him. The nurse mentioned this to me on a previous visit as, of course, it's extremely traumatizing to be shot as it does something to your psyche. Just think about hot metal piercing through your flesh, sometimes shattering bone, and there is nothing you can do to stop it. You're then in agonizing pain, bleeding out, gasping for breath when shot in the chest. Then you have to lie around while your body heals but your mind keeps reliving that particular event. I feel for him. Tonight, it seems worse than all the others, so I turn on the light and try to gently wake him. He's absolutely drenched, half of the pillow is wet and the sheets are sticking to him. I remove the sheets and straddle him. I put him in a slight bear hug and whisper for him to wake up. "Jordan, wake up." I can see his eyes rolling around behind his lids like he's looking for something. I squeeze him a little tighter and speak to him again, "Jordan, wake up." His breathing is erratic like he's re-living gasping for air after the shooting and it's starting to scare me a little. I shake him, nothing. So I come to conclusion I can't be gentle. I sit up and slap him . . . hard.

"Shit Mari, did you just slap me?!" His breathing still is not quite right.

"Sorry babe, you gave me no choice."

"I was having another nightmare, huh?"

"Yes, but this one seemed particularly bad. I couldn't wake you, so I slapped you. You want to talk about it?" I get up and motion for him to do the same so I can change the sheets. Surprisingly, he's moving around almost like his old self, as he helps me strip and re-make the bed.

"What's there to talk about, I was shot, I'm healing. Clearly, my mind didn't get the message yet. Not sure what I can say that will stop the nightmares."

"Do you remember what you dreamt once you wake up?"

"Most of the time."

"Are you re-living the day of the shooting or is it something else?"

"It's like the day of the shooting is on auto-replay or something."

"During the dream, when do you feel the most helpless?"

"The moment when I can't breathe, getting ready to black out. You're crying and I'm afraid 'our friend' is coming back to finish the job and take you. At least that how it feels."

"And I guess me telling you he snatched me into a storage closest didn't help matters?"

"Mari, I know you can take care of yourself, probably better than I ever could."

"And does that bother you?"

"Of course not!"

We finish making the bed and I stack the pillows so Jordan can sit in a reclined position. He strips his boxers off because they were soaked; I straddle him again and lie my head on his good shoulder. "Jordan, I'm not gonna pretend that I'm not pretty self-sufficient but believe me that doesn't mean I don't need you because I do. I kick myself for leaving your side when Mack shot you. I think he just waited in the wings until you were alone. Sometimes I think after the attempted mugging I stopped being aware of my surroundings, but no one can see a crazy person coming."

"I'm not sure what I'm feeling about the nightmares. I keep seeing the pain in your face when you thought I was going to die. I was out for four days, anything could have happened and I would've been helpless to stop it."

"You're worrying about stuff you don't need to. You don't even know where we are, no one does. We're safe, right?"

"I know that, tell it to my head!"

"Well aside from Hank, I'm the best partner you'll ever have. I've got your back and I know you have mine. I know you're feeling kinda vulnerable. What you went through can do that to anyone. Even you, the cop."

"I know."

"Remember when you asked me if I ever had somebody take care of me, like really care for me?"

"Yeah."

"Well, I know you have lots of family but have you ever had a female this close to you, especially in your current state of being?"

"No."

"So let me care for you Jordan." He leans over to the nightstand and grabs the gauze scissors, then hands them to me.

"Cut this shit off of me!"

"But your shoulder?!"

"Mari, cut it off; it makes me feel claustrophobic. Just grab some gauze pads and cover my wounds, but I can't sleep another night in this shit!"

I cut off the bandages. Then, I go to the bathroom to grab the gauze and tape to cover each wound individually. I start with his back. Once finished, I make him recline again against the pillows and I straddle him so I can work on the front. He still grimaces a bit when I work on his shoulder. I tell him, "I don't think this is a good idea. You're still in pain baby. Your shoulder needs to be wrapped to keep it still or at least put it in a sling." He looks at me, grabs my face, and gives me the most passionate kiss ever. Damn, I think I came a little! He grabs my night shirt and pulls it over my head. He grabs one of my breasts and puts a nipple in his mouth. God, how I've missed his touch. I can feel his hard-on spring to life beneath me. I raise up on my knees and he places his dick at my already dripping entrance.

"Geez baby you're so wet. You've missed me huh?"

"Mmmm, you have no idea how much."

"Show me."

"But your shoulder?" And what happened next ensured me I would never mention his shoulder again. He lifted me off of him. He stood up facing me, bent me over right where I was kneeling on the bed, and placed his dick back inside me. OH. MY. GOD! He feels so damn good. He leans on my back and with the good hand grabs my breast, rolling my nipple between his fingers, but with his hand on the side with the bad shoulder he reached around my waist and started rubbing my clit. He's purposely giving me a triple assault knowing I can't handle it and considering the last time we made love I'll be cuming in a matter of minutes. He strokes me and rubs my clit until I scream, and as I try to catch my breath he flips me over, drags me to the edge of the bed and licks me until I cum again. He's acting like he's just getting started when he picks up me and places me in the middle of the bed. I'm still panting when he grabs my legs and tries to put them by my ears and strokes me like nobody's business. I had to grab the bed to keep from tearing his wounds up and I think I'll need new sheets; yeah, they're definitely shredded. He came so hard, we would've been evicted from the building if we weren't on the top floor.

Needless to say, we both slept through the night in our regular position, him on his back, me cradled in his good arm, head to his heartbeat, leg across his waist, and with the death grip he loves so much.

Chapter 20

Surprisingly, I wake up before Mari and we're in a different position. That never happened before; I'm actually spooning her. We're lying on our right side with Mari's back against my chest and her plump little ass against my dick. Gives me an idea and if you never had it done to you before, you're missing out. I'm going to make Mari "cum" awake. No, it's not like having a wet dream and it's definitely not like masturbation. Orgasms are always better when they're not self-inflicted. I take my arm from around her waist to put my dick at her entrance from behind. Her back arches as I press deep inside her. Now the trick is to go slow because you don't want to wake the person; they will wake right before they explode and when they realize what is happening to them, they cum so hard, they'll be feenin' for you for days; it's like you make them a temporary nympho or something. After a few strokes, her breathing changes. I have her left breast in my right hand and I feel her nipple getting harder the more I stroke her. She starts to moan, so I kiss her softly on her neck to soothe and calm her a bit; I don't want her waking herself up with her own cries. She presses her hips back into me. Right about then, she grabs my hand from around her waist and pushes it down to rub her clit. Now we're getting somewhere. She starts to make noises again, so I suck on her neck like I'm giving her a hickey, softly, and she quiets down again. She's getting close as the pressure on my dick is absolutely insane. I pick up the pace and she's right there with me, she's so close I know she's about to wake up . . . right . . . about . . . now.

"Mmmm Jordan, what are you—? Oh God, Oh God, right there baby, right there. Mmmm, mmmm. Don't stop! Don't stop! OH GOD!"

Mari rolls over to look at me. She's breathing hard and looking at me like she wants to eat me alive. She licks her lips and pulls me in for a kiss. She grabs my dick tighter than normal, Jesus! She pushes me onto my back and slides her pussy ever so slowly down my shaft. Then, she works me like she's on a mission and it feels so goddamn good. Two more orgasms later, Mari is out like a light again and I decide to make my caretaker breakfast in bed.

She has everything you could ever want in the fridge. I wish I knew how to make those eggs Mari made the other day, but I'll stick to what I know. I make a veggie breakfast casserole with sharp cheddar. I leave the sausage out since Mari is not a big meat eater unless it's chicken or fish, and clearly I can't have any . . . yet. I'm a good boy and brown myself some more Canadian bacon and I break out the grits that I will also add the sharp cheddar to because grits aren't good without cheese! Why the big breakfast? Oh, you thought our romp from this morning was finished. NOPE! This will be an all-day session.

I make my Mari a plate. She frickin' eats like a bird. Maybe like a ¼ cup of cheesy grits and a piece of the casserole but I still cut up some fruit to place in a bowl in case she doesn't like it, pour some OJ for her and some coffee for me because I'm dying for some caffeine, then I carry the trays into the bedroom, where she's still sleeping. Hmmm . . . maybe I overdid it? I set the trays down on the dresser and walk back to the bed to gently wake her. "Wake up sleepy head. I made you breakfast."

"Hey baby? What time it is?"

"It's a little after nine."

"What did you do to me earlier? My pussy is still aching for more."

"That my love was a thank you for taking such good care of me."

"Well, let the record show, you can wake me up like that anytime. What's for breakfast? I'm starved."

79

I bring the trays over while she props herself up against the headboard. When I place the trays down, they are stacked one on top of the other. She pats the bed next to her, instructing me to sit beside her. So I take my seat and grab my tray. She asks,

"So, what's on the menu this morning?" while rubbing her hands together.

"I made my mom's breakfast casserole with cheesy grits, but I cut up some fruit for you just in case you don't like it?"

"Are you kidding? It smells wonderful," she takes a bite, "and it tastes even better. Even the coffee smells great!"

"You want some? I never see you drink coffee, but I can go make you a cup."

"I don't normally. I'd rather drink it at night over ice when I want something sweet, a little whipped cream on top."

"Hmm, that sounds good. Maybe we can have that after dinner tonight?"

"You got it! Let me get a sip of yours, it smells too good not to at least taste it."

We eat in silence for a bit, I guess we were both starving, but my food seemed to disappear faster than normal. "Hey, you ate half of mine!"

"I told you I was famished. You have no one to blame but yourself with the extracurricular activities from this morning."

"You complainin'?"

"Nope!" She starts to gather the trays. "I'll get this, you call Hank."

"I was going to call him."

"I know you were, but I was just making sure. I'll clean the kitchen, you call Hank and I want an update when I get back."

"Yes ma'am!"

I turn on my phone and of course it goes nuts again. I don't bother looking at the messages. I call Lieu.

"This is Fields, speak!"

"Hey Lieu, it's JT."

"JT, oh my God, I heard what happened. How are you?"

"I'm better than I was. Thanks for asking. How's the investigation going? Any leads on Mack?"

"Come on JT, you know I can't discuss anything about this case with you."

"I know. You don't have to give me details. I just want to know if you found him or at least have any leads."

"No we haven't found him. Speaking of which, I'm gonna email a form to you that we'll use as your statement so we can have it on file until you get a chance to swing by and sign it officially. I promise when we find him, I'll call you. Okay?"

"Thanks Lieu, I appreciate it."

"Stay safe."

"Yes ma'am."

"JT, don't ma'am me."

"Thanks Lieu, really." -- [End call]

Next, I call Hank.

"Walters."

"Hey Hank, it's JT."

"Bruh, you can't go for days at a time without letting me hear from you. You alright?"

"I'm good Hank. I was in a bad place for a bit, but I promise you I'm good now. About to start physical therapy for my shoulder actually."

"Damn JT. I've been there. Glad you made it through that shit unscathed. Being shot definitely messes with you. If you ever wanna talk you know I got you right?"

"I know man and I appreciate it. I just spoke to Lieu, she's not giving me any details. Is she sharing any particulars with you?"

"Yeah, we've been keeping in touch. You know she doesn't want to involve you at all right? So I'm the go-between. I mean you were the victim and she seems like a 'by-the-book' kind of cop."

"She is and she has to be considering her position. She's my age in a Lieutenant's position. That's no small feat."

"They followed Mack's trail on the way to you. Looks like he had a cousin who was doing Facebook Live from some bar at GCI. I checked out the video, you can clearly see you and Kamari in the background; that's how he knew where you were."

"Shit, fucking social media. I think I remember a rowdy group doing selfies. That was the first night I got here. We ended up back there after the storm because it's a place that also has screens that show arrivals and departures for the airport. You can go through security and hang out there until your flight leaves. It was the best place to be to know when the flights started back up again. Plus, the food is pretty awesome."

"I still don't get why he came after you though."

I know exactly why, but I'm not ready to let Hank in on that just yet until I figure things out. "That's a good question. I appreciate the info Hank."

"How's the little woman?"

"She's a saint, taking care of me like this. I was practically an invalid." At this point, Mari has returned and she is removing my boxers.

"You still haven't told me anything about her dude? What's the big secret?"

Mari puts my dick in her mouth and I'm having a tough time keeping my composure. "Hank. I—um, we'll have to talk about, sssss that at, *shit Mari*, another time."

"Bruh, I can take a hint. You sure she doesn't have a sister? You lucky bastard!"

"Ssss, Hank, I promise you . . . she . . . does not . . . have . . . a sister. I'll call you, *sssshit*, in a couple of days." [End call]. "You are, ssss sooo doing this . . . on purpose." Mari says,

"I have an itch I need you to scratch."

Chapter 21

Kamari

       I purposely yank Jordan's boxers off while he's on the phone with Hank. He created this horny monster, though I'm sure that was his plan. I push him off of the pillows and sucked the color off his dick. I practically had him howling.

"Shit Mari, I think I need oxygen."

"I can give you mouth to mouth."

"No, I need to catch my breath; the physical therapist will be here in about an hour."

"Aww, so we can't take a shower before your session?"

"I would love a repeat shower romp but if I go in there with you, I'll have nothing left for PT."

"Ok, I'll let you off the hook this time. Before you take your shower 'alone,' did Hank tell you anything about Mack?"

"Yeah, GC and Reno PD haven't found him yet, but Hank said Mack found us because his cousin was fucking doing Facebook Live and you could see us clearly in the background."

"Wow, what are the chances of that?"

"Small world babe."

"I'm sorry Jordan."

"Sorry? For what?"

"For one, almost getting you killed!"

"Come on baby, you can't possibly feel guilty about Mack's actions."

"Well, I used him."

"I have a feeling he agreed to everything you offered, thinking he could convince you of more."

"Yeah." I kiss him. "Go take your shower. Everything is setup in the training room. I'll make you a sandwich to have after your session."

"Oh my God since I'm working out now can a brotha at least have some bacon on his sandwich, some real bacon?!"

"Geez, you big baby. I'll make you a club sandwich, okay? Double decker."

"Bet!"

Chapter 22

JT

After my physical therapy session, of course my shoulder is killing me and I didn't even work with weights yet. I'll be on resistance bands for the first two weeks, then weights on the remaining two. Plus, the therapist has me doing jump rope for 30 minutes to re-build my lung capacity. The therapist wrapped an ice pack on my shoulder before releasing me for the day. I walked her out because Mari was MIA. I walk into the kitchen still smelling the bacon Mari cooked earlier for my sandwich. I have to laugh at myself; I never wanted bacon so bad before in my life. Mari has my sandwich sitting on the counter with some lemonade and French fries, not as much as I would want, so I get what she's doing. Surprisingly, I don't see her as we normally eat all our meals together. I go to the fridge to grab ketchup and that's when I see her sitting in the living room. She has headsets on, so she doesn't hear me moving around in the kitchen, and by looking at the screen, I can see why with all the chaos going on. Wait a minute, is that Black Ops 4? *SHIT*, it's not even out yet. How the hell does she have it already?! I grab my sandwich and drink (*screw the ketchup*) and go over to the sofa where she's sitting. That's when she notices me.

"Hey baby, all done?" She says removing the headset from her ear on the side I'm sitting. Now I see she has a sandwich on the table in front of her with fries and a small bowl of ketchup (*good, now I don't have to make a trip back to the kitchen*).

"Yeah, how in the hell do you have Black Ops 4 already?"

"Oh, I signed up years ago to be one of the beta testers, thinking I would never get picked and then I did. I love these games."

"Damn, give me a controller. Let's do split screen!"

"You don't wanna eat first?"

"I can multitask. Hurry up before the next game loads so I can sign into my account."

"No rush, I can back out so you can setup. Plus, I didn't want to eat until you were done, so I decided to play to kill time."

I take two extremely large bites of my sandwich, stuff 3 or 4 fries into my mouth after dipping them in her ketchup, and took a big gulp of the lemonade right before she tosses me the controller.

"How long are you supposed to keep the ice pack on?"

"Ummm, like 20 minutes." After I get logged into my account, I start setting up my rollout. I'll have to work with the basics until I can get better weapons.

"You don't want a shower first so you can really relax?"

"If you think I'm gonna shower while you build your BO4 skills without me, you're crazy."

"You do realize we'll be on the same team, right?"

"Thank God, because if you play beta the way you fight, I would be screwed!"

"I can hold my own."

For the next several hours, Mari and I play BO4 on split screen like we've been partners for years. She even frickin' snipes like nobody's business; she's a quick scope queen from the word go!! Personally, I like up-close-and-personal battle, like a shotgun to the face, a hatchet to the chest, or getting two or more enemies in a room with one grenade. We end up playing until dark and you can actually hear our stomachs growling over all the explosions on the screen. I think we only stopped long enough to do a bathroom break and grab something else to drink. I don't even remember Mari removing the ice pack from my shoulder. Yeah, we've got it kinda bad. She looks at me and says,

"You ready to eat?"

"Yeah, let me give you a hand though."

"That'll work."

"Whatcha making?"

"I figured you're finally ready for a steak."

"And what will you be having?"

"Bourbon salmon."

"Well hell Mari, that sounds better than the steak."

"Tell you what; I'll give your steak the bourbon glaze, so you don't feel like you're missing out."

"Sounds like a plan, what can I do to assist?"

"You make the salad, and I'll put potatoes on for the cheddar mash."

"Oh man, steak and potatoes. You're spoiling me sweetheart!"

"Don't forget I'm making the iced coffee with whipped cream for dessert."

"You really trying to make sure I don't leave aren't ya?"

"Is it working?"

"Like you have to ask."

88

After all the food is prepared, I grab myself a beer and a glass of wine for Mari. We take a seat at the dining room table where I decide to hammer out a few things before we get to the point when we actually leave the comfort of this place.

"Hey baby, you do realize in a few weeks I'll have to go back to Reno and Ellensburg to wrap things up?"

"Yeah, I know. And you realize that I'm not leaving your side from this point forward, right?"

"Hey, I'm no fool. By your side is the safest place to be, especially with Mack still out there. So we need a plausible reason why you're with me so it doesn't look suspicious."

"Agreed and I'm sure you already have something in mind."

"Yeah. You'll be my protection detail."

"Isn't protection detail normally done by another cop?"

"Normally, but since I technically work for myself as a consultant, I can contract an outside agency for protection and bill the department since I was on duty at the time of the attack. Not that I would bill them in this case."

"I like the idea of being your bodyguard, gives me a reason to beat people up."

"Slow your roll momma, this is serious. You have to present yourself a particular way for it to be believable and wear sunglasses so no one picks up on how you look at me."

"How do I look at you?"

"The same way I look at you, like you want to eat me or something. And on that note, stay out of my line of sight or I'll never be able concentrate on what I need to do. Stay in close proximity to me, say . . . close enough to get to me if you have to but far enough away to where you can't hear me speaking to someone else."

"Got it."

"You got a black suit you can wear?"

"Yes."

"And pin your hair up in a teacher's bun or something."

"I know just the getup. Am I allowed to talk to anyone, not that I want to?"

"I'll leave that up to you as you know the places we're going are mostly guys, so you're gonna get hit on. I'll let you handle that at your own discretion, just don't break any bones."

"Will them hitting on me bother you?"

"You just want me to say it out loud, don't cha?" She gives me the most adorable smile.

"Just wondering how you feel about it, that's all."

"You're really getting a kick out of this aren't you? Yes, it will bother me, which is another reason why I don't want you in my line of sight, not sure if I'll be able to keep my composure. We'll have to go to Reno first since that's Mack's city of residence. I have to physically sign my statement. Just a heads up, the Lieutenant is female, the other reason for your sunglasses. I don't want anyone noticing whatever eye daggers you'll be throwing her way. Plus, I'm not sure how much experience you have around other women." Her facial expression changes like she's becoming jealous already. I grab her hand, "Mari, the only person I'm interested in is you. Lieu is a higher-ranking officer, so

I would never go down that road anyway. No worries, okay." She takes a deep breath and says,

"Okay. I'll call ahead to have the jet on standby. How long we staying?"

"Just a day or two. I'm going strictly for the paperwork. Lieu will forward the signed paperwork to GCPD for their records since the incident happened there. Then when we return, we can drive down to see Hank as I need to talk to him about something, and it's not something you can do over the phone, no matter how clean our phones happen to be."

"Understood. Is that it? You ready for dessert?"

"Yeah, I'ma grab a shower while you do that." She grabs my hand before I get up.

"Nope, I'll put the coffee on and *we'll* grab a shower. You eighty-sixed my shower with you this morning, remember?"

"Oh yeah, well after you babe."

Chapter 23

Kamari

Jordan is 100% back to normal. He finished up his PT, his appetite is back to normal, and his stamina is better than I remember. Our bags are packed and the jet is ready when we are. I didn't even try the bun Jordan suggested; I have too much hair for that. So I just go with a tightly braided single braid that I wrap around itself and pinned down. I wrap a black ribbon around it and made it look like a bow tie to go with the outfit. I'm wearing skin-tight leggings so I can wear my hip-high black leather boots, skin-tight, low-cut shirt with a collar for my tie that goes over my breasts to hide the cleavage but shows just a little skin with a suit jacket that pulls in at the waist. Surprisingly, it's a very comfortable outfit. I walk out of the bathroom into the bedroom when Jordan's jaw drops and he says,

"Oh hell no! You're not wearing that!"

"What? It's a black suit."

"That is in no way, shape, or form a black suit. Come on Mari, how am I supposed to concentrate on what I'm doing with you looking like that?"

"I'll be out of your line of sight, remember?" I slide my sunglasses on and quote Will Smith from the MIB movie, "I make this look good!"

"Shit, you bring attention to yourself wearing that. Are those fuckin' knives in your boots?!"

"Good, that takes the attention off you, which is the job right? And to answer your question, yes, I always wear knives. Plus, I can wear a trash bag and some guy will still hit on me. I have to wear a disguise to go grocery shopping just to keep from getting hit on. I want to look nice for you."

"You look fuckin' amazing! I feel sorry for the guy that hits on you today. Just don't break any bones, well . . . unless he deserves it."

***

We get to the station in Reno and I'm on Jordan's six trying to keep my wits about me as Jordan's cologne is filling my nostrils making me think of all the naughty things I want to do to him when we get back home. We walk through the station to the Lieutenant's office where she steps out. You can tell she's happy to see Jordan, and I'm just not sure how I feel about that. Then, she notices me. She taps Jordan on his shoulder instructing him to her office, while walking straight over to me and introduces herself with an outstretched hand.

"I'm Lieu." I can feel her business card in my hand when I grab hers. "I'm glad you're detailing Thompson. If things get hairy, my personal number is on the back." I lower my glasses to look her in the eyes and for some reason I wink at her but I choose not to speak. Surprisingly, she took the initiative to speak to me first before Jordan and I respect the hell out of that. She continues, "Oh and considering some of the people who work for me, you have my permission to break bones if anyone gets out of line with you." I smile a really big smile after she says that. I like her!

***

JT
I watch the exchange between Lieu and Mari, and it has me nervous as shit especially when I see the biggest smile I've ever seen on Mari's face. They walk together to the office, but Mari stops short of the door outside and Lieu closes it when she enters. When Lieu hands me some paperwork, I ask,

"What the hell did you say to her? I don't think I've ever seen her smile like that."

"That's between me and your girl."

"And why do you call her that?"

"Come on JT, I can see it on you both. I can tell she kicks serious ass too. That girl's a fighter!"

"How can you even tell that?!"

"A woman that dresses like that brings out the stupidity in others, which in turn will be their downfall. I can't wait until Jenkins walks in and sees her. He's had it coming for 5 years."

"Jesus woman! What the fuck are you talking about now?"

"Jenkins is a guy that felt he should've gotten the Lieutenant's job. He didn't mind letting me know it either. I broke several of his fingers and suspended him twice, but didn't have the heart to fire him."

"Why not? Sounds like he deserves to be."

"Oh he does, but give someone enough rope and they'll hang themselves. I'm sure his third strike is coming up."

As soon as the words left Lieu's mouth, I hear a commotion outside of the office. When I turn around, I see a guy flying through the air and Mari scrambling to the top of a desk, jump in the air, and landing on said guy right when his back hits the floor. We run out of the office and up to Mari where she has the same guy pinned under her and he's screaming like she already broke something. FUCK! Lieu speaks only to the guy at this point.

"What the fuck did you do Jenkins?!"

"Get her off me, she's crazy! I think she broke my arm! Get her the fuck off me!"

I'm standing there in shock because this guy is just as big as Mack, a bit bigger than me and Mari knocked him on his ass and broke his arm, which I specifically told her not to do unless . . . SHIT! I tap Mari on the shoulder and she immediately let's go and gets up, taking her place behind me. I ask Lieu,

"What happened?"

"Stupid fucker probably put his hands on her. Johnson, take ditmo to the ER."

Lieu gets up and walks over to Mari to look her over, not that she needs to, and asks "You need to press charges?" Mari answers,

"No, he's been punished enough."

I ask Lieu if I can borrow her office and she just waves her hand at me. I look at Mari and tell her "Office, now!"

After we get in the office, Mari removes her sunglasses and takes her protection stance in case someone is watching, waiting for me to say something. "What the fuck happened out there?"

"He touched me."

"Where?"

"He was sticking his business card in my breast pocket that I don't have!"

"Did you have to break his arm?"

"Yes, the one he used to touch me. Plus, I had confirmed permission."

"What the hell does that mean?"

"You told me don't break any bones unless the person deserved it. Then, Lieu gave me explicit permission to break the bones of anyone that gets out of line with me."

"Shit! That's what you were smiling about? She knew that guy was going to hit on you; she broke his fingers before herself. Do you actually enjoy hurting people?"

"Of course not! He had no right to put his hands on me. I've had guys touch me before and they all survived okay?! Usually, they just grab my hand to keep me from walking away. No one grabs my ass or touches my breast, and I'm definitely not going to let them get away with it when they do."

At that point, Lieu walks back into her office and Mari puts her sunglasses back on, but I can tell she's going to chew me a new one when we're finally alone.

Chapter 24

Kamari

On the way back to the jet, I didn't speak a word and I think Jordan was too scared to say anything for fear of setting me off. He hurt me when he asked if I enjoy hurting people, but I'm an assassin, or at least I was. When I performed a hit, I didn't hate it, but I didn't revel in it either. Is he having second thoughts about me? We come from such different backgrounds, I take life and he's into protecting it.

We embark on the jet to take our seats and as I walk past him, he grabs my hand and pulls me into his lap. I assume my regular position, straddling his lap with my head in the crook of his neck when he speaks while rubbing my back.

"I'm sorry baby. I thought he hurt you and I wanted to fuckin' break his other arm and wrap my hands around his goddamn throat! I thought talking to you to find out exactly what happened would cool me off but I wanted to look you over and make sure you were okay, and I couldn't do that in front of everyone, which pissed me off even more. I know you don't like hurting people and my heart sank as soon as the words left my mouth and I—"

I breathed a sigh of relief and I reached up to his face to pull him down to kiss me. Now I understand his reaction. He wanted to hold me and in that moment he couldn't. How would it look if he was hugging his protection detail? I'm supposed to be hired protection not his girlfriend. This is going to be harder than I thought. Maybe the cops in Ellensburg will have more restraint.

***

We get back to our place. WOW, did I just say *our* place? Okay, let me try that again. We get back home feeling like we've been gone an entire week when it's only been two days. It seems this particular outing has me all in my head again. It was easier

97

to be a couple when we were in a place where no one knew us. Now that I'm slowly being integrated into Jordan's world it seems to be an adjustment. I guess that makes sense, as before Jordan, I really didn't deal with anyone accept for the occasional booty call and that was brief, like one and done. Considering the situation, what becomes of Jordan and me when Mack is caught, do I become Suzy Homemaker and belt out a couple of kids while Jordan goes to work? Yeah, I have plenty of money stashed away so it's not like I actually *have* to work but what do I do with myself? I'm actually feeling kind of lost. At this point, Jordan grabs me from behind and pulls me into a hug; how does he know when I need to be held? He asks,

"What's the matter babe?"

"I'm just wondering what becomes of us when all of this is over."

"What do you mean, 'what becomes of us'? You not planning on bailing on me are you?"

"Of course not. I mean. Geez . . . let's talk about the other elephant in the room. I kill people for a living Jordan. Clearly, that's not something I can continue to do if I plan on staying with you."

"Come with me." We walk into the bedroom. Jordan stacks several pillows on the bed, so he can sit in a reclined position. He holds his hand out and I grab it. I know the drill. I straddle his lap and lie against his chest. I'm not sure why, but this just seems to be the way we talk. It's extremely calming, voices are never raised, but I think he does it for me more than anything. It just feels like the safest place in the world to be. He continues the conversation. "First things first, do you plan on staying with me?"

I sit up. "Oh my God, do you really need to ask that?"

"I have to know exactly what you're thinking babe so we can hammer out the rest."

98

"Yes, you couldn't get rid of me even if you tried."

"Do you have any interest in taking a job at this point?"

"No, I haven't even thought about work in that way, only what do I do with myself if taking contracts is something I'm no longer doing."

"Let's cross that bridge when we get to it. We're both dealing with a lot at the moment. Let's take care of the threat first, then we can deal with the rest. I'm sure we can figure out something we can both agree with."

"Ok, well how about on a more permanent note. You're still living out of a suitcase. Don't you think you need to have your things sent here already?"

He now sits up, grabs my face to lean his forehead against mine, then kisses my forehead ever so slightly. "Already packed babe, was just waiting for your okay."

"Really? If I had known it was that easy and where your stuff was, I would've had your things sent here those four days you were unconscious."

"Just waiting for you to feel comfortable enough to broach the subject, love."

"I truly appreciate you allowing me to go at my own pace."

"Anything for you babe, just be up front with me especially with how you're feeling. I don't want you stewing in your own juices and misconstruing something. Got it?"

"You picked up on that huh?"

"I admit—I didn't handle the situation all that well either. This entire situation is all kinds of fucked up, makes it hard to handle like a regular, everyday state of affairs. We're definitely gonna have to get our shit together before Ellensburg, especially since Hank has met you and I haven't given him any details about you. I'm not even sure if I'm gonna let him into the circle. I'm still soaking on that."

"Jordan, I love you."

"I love you too baby. Come on, let's get some sleep. Maybe we'll push the Ellensburg trip back a day or two until we figure some other things out, like you needing a different suit."

"Really?"

"Oh I'm not joking."

I get up to take my clothes off while Jordan watches me undress. "Tell you what. I will actually let you pick out my outfit if you can make me cum before I make you cum."

"Hmm . . . 69? Bet!"

Needless to say, I lost that bet!

Chapter 25

JT

I wake up again alone in bed hearing the thumping in the distance. I know what it is, but the question is, why is it going on this time? Mari gets up early to kick the shit out of the punching bag when something is bothering her and considering the conversation we had last night, she should be good . . . right? I get up to check on her. I glance at the clock this time . . . 5 a.m. again. I walk across the penthouse to the exercise room and there she is kicking the bag but I'm noticing that the bag is actually falling apart. It wasn't like this the other day, which means she is royally pissed about something. Considering how the bag looks and the look on her face, I know better than to disturb her; I'll just sit here until she's finished. She does a roundhouse to the bag, detaching it completely from where it was hanging. It ends up in a pile on the floor and she looks around the room like she needs to do something else. She picks up some mini blades and starts throwing them at a wooden target and I mean her accuracy is fuckin' scary. Every single one is a head shot or a heart shot, some hit removing the last blade thrown. When she runs out of blades she looks around again and that's when she sees me. Lucky for me, her demeanor softens like all she needed was to see my face to be alright. She walks up to me and hugs me, extremely tight. I ask her,

"What's wrong babe? Whose face are you seeing?"

"Fucking Mack!"

"What happened between last night and this morning?"

"My primary phone went off this morning. It was an alarm notification from the cabin."

"You're fuckin' kidding me?!"

"No. I literally got up, got dressed and was about to walk out the door but as soon as I grabbed the doorknob I couldn't leave, like something was pulling me, keeping me from leaving. I can't explain it. When I realized I wasn't going to leave you behind I was too wound up to go back to sleep, so I decided to punch the ever loving shit out of my bag. I guess I need a new one now."

"I guess it would be stupid of me to ask what exactly you were going to do once you got to the cabin."

"Oh I was going to kill him. No doubt about it and it was going to be painful. I told him if I ever found him I would be the last thing he saw. I didn't think the fucker would break into my cabin."

"Well considering he's on the run, that is the perfect place to hide, knowing you probably weren't there."

"Let me take care of him Jordan. I'll be back before you even miss me."

"No. It's not like you really need my permission, and it's not like I can stop you either."

"I know, but I promised you I wouldn't take matters into my own hands, so I need you to release me from that so I can end it."

"No. I'm struggling with this too Mari. I'm trying to wrap this all up in a nice and neat little bow, which goes against my nature, so you have to do the same. And for the record, I would miss you as soon as you walked out that door and surely wouldn't let you go at it alone. We're partners now, no going off half-cocked. You got me?"

"Yes sir!" she said with a sexy smirk.

***

I finally decide to let Hank in on the secret. My problem is, is that even fair to do to him or Mari? I discuss it with Mari first before I make any moves.

"Hey babe, let me holler at you for a sec."

"Yeah, what's up?"

"I was thinking about telling Hank about what we're dealing with. I think we're gonna need his help."

"Are you guys close enough that you feel you can trust him with this?"

"I would like to think so. We've been working together longer than I've known you and I think we're like brothers, but that can spin on a dime with the shit I'm about to drop on him."

"Well considering how your shooting affected him, I would say he would do anything for you."

"Really? Why do you say that?"

"When he came to the hospital to see you, I could tell he wanted to kill someone for you, but he also had a lot of hurt in his eyes for the state you were in."

"Hmm. Pack a bag babe. Road trip!"

***

We leave almost immediately since we're only two hours away. I want to speak to Hank in person and not at the station for obvious reasons. About 10 minutes out from Hank's place, I shoot him a text to see if he's home or still at the station.

> Me: Hank where u @
> Hank: On my way home 2 order sum Chinese, what's up

Me: On my way 2 u, b there in 10
Hank: Doesn't sound like a social visit, u alright
Me: Yes and no
Hank: ? I'm 5 mins out, c u in a bit

Mari pulls up into Hank's driveway. When we exit the car, Hank opens the door and steps out onto the porch. Mari was right. He's looking at me like he just found his long lost brother and embraces me.

"Wow bruh, missed me?"

"Like you have to ask. You had me thinking for a minute I wouldn't see your face again. Hello Kamari, glad you didn't completely disappear with my brother here."

Mari says, "You know he wouldn't be too far from you."

"Come on in. You guys ate? I can add you to the pot."

"I thought you were ordering Chinese because I know you're not cooking."

"Uh duh. Just wanna know if I need to add yall to the order."

"Sure, anything with veggies and chicken or fish for Mari and I'll have what you're having."

Hank does several taps on the screen of his phone. Geez, is there really an app for everything? He tosses the phone on the coffee table and gives me the once over, then lays into me a wee bit.

"Not that I'm not glad to see you but why has it taken so fucking long to lay eyes on you. You don't even call a brotha. Not to sound like a girl but I've been worried about you man. What's up?"

"Sorry Hank, being off the grid was a necessity, not just for my safety but I needed time to heal. Plus, I had to wrap my head around A LOT of things over the past few weeks." He follows my eyes as I look at Mari who's standing at the storm door looking out, like actually being a lookout, being overprotective.

"Ok, get me up to speed."

"First I need to know. If I was in trouble, could I count on you to help me fix it, even if it's off the books?"

"Yeah."

"I'm serious Hank. What's going on with me is not cool but I need to do it in order to protect someone I care for . . . deeply." I look at Mari again and Hank watches me look at her.

"JT, just ask."

At that moment, a car pulls up in the driveway and Mari is out the door quicker than necessary. Hank is a bit startled how fast she moved. I call out to her, "It's just the Chinese delivery Mari, don't break any bones." I follow Hank to the door as he's watching her. She has her knee on the door to keep the person from exiting the vehicle while she receives the food through the window and pays. She stands on the grass until the person is completely out of the driveway and you can no longer hear the car as it turns off the street before she walks back to the house. I sit down at the table; Hank backs up as Mari walks by him bags in hand. She says, "You ready to eat?" Hank says,

"What the hell was that?"

"That my friend is my protection detail."

"She moved like a frickin' ninja when she went out the door!"

Mari just smiles proudly, fixes her food and sits at the counter between the kitchen and dining area. Then I notice Hank's eyes become extremely huge.

"Bruh, that's the chick from the bar!!!"

"What?"

Hank grabs me by my good shoulder to make me stand, turns me around to face Mari sitting on the stool with her back to us when I have a flashback to the first night he and I were in the bar looking at this same silhouette sitting at the bar turning guys away left and right. *Well I'll be damned*!

"Holy shit, I'm right? It is her isn't it? I'd remember that ass anywhere."

As soon as the words left Hank's mouth I held my arms up as I knew Mari was about to get up without thinking. Before I knew it, she was in front of both of us giving Hank the evil eye.

"Sorry sugar . . . I did more staring back on that day; today's glance was just a confirmation."

"Sorry Hank, reflex. I know you wouldn't disrespect me, especially in front of Jordan."

"Alright JT spill."

I give Hank the complete story of everything that happened, who Mari is, how she's the root of the majority of my cases, how we met, why Mack attacked me; the whole nine. Needless to say, he looks a little . . . shell shocked.

"So let me get this straight. This little lady is a drop-dead, gorgeous killer-for-hire? In fact, actually a ninja, who kicks ass and makes guys fall in love with her to the point where the one before you tried to kill you to have her to himself??!!! Where's Ashton Kutcher? Am I being 'Punked'?"

Mari and I stare at Hank to give him a second to realize we are dead serious. He's looking back and forth between us.

"You're both serious?"

"YES!" Mari and I say in unison.

"I don't buy it. You'll never convince me this little thing is a hired killer. What is she like a buck-o-five?"

Mari answers him amused. "115 actually, without gear."

"Gear?"

Mari gives him a smirk. The interaction between them is hilarious. I'm just gonna watch. I have a feeling Hank is about to get a lesson he won't soon forget.

"I need a demonstration. Let's hit the backyard."

"Hank, full disclosure. I would not in any way, shape or form even play fight with Mari. As a matter of fact, I'm about to ask for some lessons." Mari gives me an excited smile. "You do this at your own risk."

"You're shitting me."

I look at Mari like I'm pleading with her. She just smiles at me, grabs my hand as we all walk to the backyard. She rises up on her tippy toes to give me a kiss and tells me "I promise I won't hurt him, babe." I breathe a sigh of relief.

"JT, you look a little nervous."

"This is between you and her bruh, but if it's any consolation, I don't want to watch but I have to."

"Damn bruh, now I'm nervous."

Mari chimes in, "Don't be, I promised Jordan I wouldn't hurt you." Hank busts out laughing.

"You, hurt me?! Ok, this is going to be interesting."

I decide to make some ground rules. "Ok guys, because I don't want to see anyone hurt, *feelings not included*, let me make some rules. Mari DO NOT break any bones, no fractures, no sprains, no strains, NO Kyuusho. Hank good luck."

"Bruh, no rules for me? I'm offended!"

"Hank, with all the nos I just gave Mari, you'll thank me."

Hank decides to egg Mari on. "Ok Kamari, show me what you got. In the words of Morpheus from The Matrix . . . 'hit me, if you can'." As soon as he said the words, Mari sweeps Hank's legs from under him, landing him on his back. "Shit!"

Mari extends a hand to Hank to help him up. Once he's upright she tells him. "Ok Hank, I'm gonna go for your torso including your stomach or your back, nothing over your heart, don't want to stop it." Hank's face has a little fear on it when it registers that Mari can stop his heart with a blow to his chest. "You think you can stop me?"

"I guess we'll find out in a bit."

Mari backs up and starts to circle Hank; personally, I think she's doing it to intimidate him a bit but he's keeping his front facing her as she moves. She takes off toward him and he widens his stance. Once he plants his feet Mari dashes through his legs feet first. He tries to grab her on the way through but she did it so fast, he was already too late. Now, his butt is in the air with his arms reaching between his legs and that's when Mari stops her slide by grabbing his arms taking him with her, almost pulling him through his own legs and onto his back, again; she daintily taps his chest for good measure. It's fuckin' hilarious, like something off The Three Stooges. She puts out her hand again to help him up and tells him,

"You wanna go again?"

"You're a quick little minx aren't ya?"

"Yeah, but you're also slow."

          Shit, why did she say that? Now she's trying to get into Hank's head. I don't think he'll be easily baited unless his pride is hurt, and it doesn't help that he's been on his back twice already. I speak up, "Guys, I think we should stop playing and start strategizing on the matter at hand."

"Nah bruh, I can take her."

"Hank, I can't even take her. She's getting into your head, don't fall for it." At that point, Mari pulls out a scarf, covers her eyes, and turns her back to Hank. *SHIT*! Hank looks at me like he has to try one more time. While shaking my head 'no', I mouth the words to him *it's a trap*, but he ignores me and runs toward her lunging. She side-steps him, does a roundhouse to his back and right before he falls, she grabs him at his belt to keep him from doing a face plant into the dirt. She removes her blindfold, looks at Hank and says,

"We good Hank?"

"Shit Kamari, I know you don't have a sister, got any cousins?" She pulls him upright.

"Sorry, I'm an only child to parents who also had no siblings."

109

Once Hank is on his own two feet, he holds out his arms and says, "Consider yourself no longer just JT's but you're my family now too lil sis!" I can see the emotion in Mari's eyes. She embraces him and they both walk back over to me with an arm around each other smiling.

"You guys good. We not breaking up the band, right?"

Hank gives me a big smile, some dap, and says "We're good. I get it. She's a keeper. Shit, put me down for a few lessons too Kam." Both Mari and I look at Hank weirdly and say together,

"Kam?!"

"Yeah, Kamari sounds too formal and Mari sounds like JT's special name for you. So since we're family, you need a nickname; and there is nothing better than a nickname that sounds like a boy's name for a girl who kicks ass."

Mari looks like she's actually mulling it over before speaking and says, "Hmm, I like it!"

Chapter 26

Kamari

After me and Hank's fight session, we all hit the sack. Jordan wants to leave as soon as we wake to go back home with Hank meeting up with us later after he puts in for time off. Jordan and I chat in bed for a bit before falling asleep.

"Jordan? Do you have a game plan yet?"

"I got a few things worked out, but not all of it. I don't like Mack being at the cabin. I don't want anything leading back to you other than trying to use his obsession for you to our advantage."

"Hmm, sounds interesting."

"Yeah, gonna need a bit more time to work out the kinks and in the meantime, Mack could take off again."

"Why not just use me as bait? I can take a trip to the cabin and pretend I don't know he's there, give him a chance to follow me or something."

"Absolutely not! I'm not leaving you alone with him. We don't even know his state of mind since you threatened him. You might be on his shit list along with me now. Too risky babe."

"I can handle him."

"I know you can babe but you're not Neo, this is not The Matrix. You're fast, but you can't dodge bullets."

"Mostly at point-blank range . . ."

Jordan looks at me with astonishment, opens his mouth to say something, then closes it, like a fish out of water. He gives up by shaking his head.

$***$

JT

I'm awakened by slight jiggling. When I open my eyes, it's Hank with his finger over his lips and nodding his head towards the door telling me to come with him quietly. Once outside of the bedroom, I ask yawning, "What's with the stealth exit."

"I didn't want to wake Kam."

"Too late, she jiggled me before you did. I'm sure she woke up as soon as you turned the knob. What's up?"

"Damn her ninja hearing, my bad. Gotta text from Lieu. Mack was spotted on camera coming back to the States from Canada but they lost sight of him several miles in."

"Where did he cross? Did she say?"

"Yeah, Washington."

"Shit, I wonder if Mari—"

At that point, Mari comes out of the room to join the conversation. No doubt she's been listening the entire time. She says,

"No, there is nothing in the cabin that can be traced back to me including the deed. Him crossing into the Washington can just be a coincidence or easy access from his starting point."

I tell her, "Or he can be coming to Washington for something specific and if it's not you then who or what?"

Hank says, "A way to get to her."

112

Mari has this look on her face and she's looking at Hank like they're communicating without talking. Then she says, "It's almost time to get up anyway. Hank, do your thing at the office and text Jordan when you're about 20 minutes out from Seattle, then I'll have him send you the address. Jordan and I are leaving." She's looking at me "Right now!"

***

Mari and I are in the car with her driving. I'm looking at her and she looks different. I can't tell what I'm seeing in her but I don't like it. "Mind letting me in on the secret?"

"Jordan," she grabs my hand. "Mack is coming for me and he is going to use either you or Hank to do it. Hank agreed to be bait."

"WHAT!? You two just decided without saying anything to me. Hell, neither one of you even spoke a word. What the fuck was that about?"

"Sorry babe, he gets it. You are trying so hard to protect me when it's you who actually needs protecting."

"I'm trying to keep you from being punished for your past killings."

"I know you are babe and that pales in comparison to live in a world without you in it. I want you to know being introduced to your world has been quite an adjustment and I'm truly struggling with it. Now you are about to be pulled into mine and you're not gonna to like it."

"Why, what's going on?"

"I can't explain it, call it a hunch but I think Mack has tracked you to Ellensburg. He has to go through you to get to me and I'm absolutely not going to let that happen. I'm not sure if he saw us arrive or leave Hank's or not but I guarantee you Hank is his way to get to you."

"Shit Mari and we left him behind unprotected! We have to go back!"

"Jordan, do you trust me?"

"Of course but—"

"But nothing! Do you trust Hank?"

"Of course!"

"You will do as I say without question. Everything I will do is for your safety as Mack's goal is to get you out of the way."

"This is way out of my comfort zone Mari."

"I know it is and I've been in that place for a while. I suggest you meet me there and get comfortable. You're in my world now."

My phone goes off with an incoming text.

Hank: Your delivery has been rerouted

There's a picture attached with Hank tied up in the back of a trunk, then another text comes through.

Hank: Bring me what I want and you can have him back, no cops

"SHIT! How did we get here?!"

Chapter 27

Mack

I've been trying to figure out for weeks how to get Mar to come to me and I finally came up with a plan. It didn't dawn on me until I opened my wallet and saw that fucker's business card with his contact information on it. I forgot I even had it. I called the main line as I didn't want to speak with him directly. I asked for his whereabouts stating I had information on one of his cases and wanted to speak with him in person. Due to our previous encounter, he is considered on leave. So, like a normal person I asked to speak to whomever he was working with and was given the name of Henry Walters. I arrive at the Ellensburg Police Department and in the foyer on the wall I see a photo of the same guy for some award he received. Now that I know what he looks like, I go back to my car and wait.

He's here extremely early even by police standards I would say, but what do I know? He's inside maybe 30 minutes before he is back out and in his car. I follow him to what I assume is his house. I don't see any other cars so I take my chance when he comes out to get in his car, small duffle bag in hand.

"Going somewhere?"

"Apparently, considering you're pointing a gun at me; otherwise, I'd be dead already."

"True. Let's go. I'll give you a ride." I walk him to the back of my car and pop the trunk. He turns around to look at me.

"Come on man, do you really want to go through all this for some chick."

I crack him across the face. "DON'T CALL HER THAT! Give me your phone and put your ass in the trunk!" He steps inside and I crack him again on the back of his head knocking

x

115

him out cold. I tie him up for good measure and use his phone to snap a photo. I text my friend to let him know plans have changed.

Chapter 28

JT

We get back home and Mari immediately starts pulling out weaponry and a few bags. She looks at me and says, "Pack for a fight." I go to our bedroom and start packing all my gear, guns, clips, bullets, burner phones, etc. I hear Mari on the phone and she's speaking Japanese. I throw some clothes in a duffle bag and put my things by the door. I come into the kitchen and she's . . . cooking? I say,

"I'm not hungry."

"Well, we're both going to need to eat but this isn't food. I'm making a fresh batch of poison."

"Why the fresh batch, don't you have some already on hand?"

"Yeah but this batch has no plasma in it. I need Mack's blood to get the plasma to add to this one."

I'm just looking at her because I have no idea where she is going with this and then she says,

"I'm going to add his plasma to the poison, then you can do whatever you need to do to replace my DNA in the police database with his."

Then Mari really shocks me when she pulls out a business card, I don't know whose, and makes a call.

"Lieu, it's Kamari. Things just got hairy."

I listen to her one-sided conversation with her just saying a bunch of yeahs, nos, and uh huhs before she hangs up. Then I ask her,

"Mari, what the fuck is going on?"

"Contingency plan to give you deniability. When this is all over, I need you to be able to continue to be you without any repercussions."

"And why do you, Lieu and Hank get to make that decision for me? How's that fair?"

"First of all, Hank took time off, so no one knows he's been grabbed but you and me. Lieu is going to do her job; she's just giving me a window to get my shit done before she takes over."

"Jesus, why does it feel like I'm a kid being given a timeout or something?"

"This is what it feels like to have several people care about you. My goal is to eliminate the threat so I can have that too on a regular basis."

"Fine. What do you need me to do?"

"We're going to get a room at one of the motels closest to the cabin. When we get close, you're going to stay in the car and wait for Hank to come out. I won't leave the cabin until Hank is out of harm's way. You two will then go back to the motel and wait for me there."

"You're insane if you think I'm going to leave you alone with him!"

"Jordan, you will do as I ask. You have been on my trail for a while, I'm a killer and I have to be that killer again for all this to end, and I'm willing to do that to keep you safe."

"Mari . . ."

"Jordan, if you want me to remain in your life there are things you should not see me doing, and this is one of them. You only have a glimpse of what I'm capable of and I don't want to taint your idea of me."

"Baby, I know exactly who you are." I bring her into my arms and kiss her softly. "You are the love of my life, the best partner I've ever had and definitely the better half of this relationship. Considering the lengths you're taking to keep me safe only proves who you are to me and you couldn't taint that if you tried."

"Wow, you have no idea how good that makes me feel." She says as I wipe a tear from her eye. "I may have killed for money, but I would wipe anyone off the face of the Earth for free if they tried to take you from me."

"I have no doubts about that."

"We good?"

"Yeah baby, let's go get Hank. I swear, if Mack harms you, I'm not going to be responsible for my actions."

"It won't come to that. Let's go."

Chapter 29

Kamari

We get to the motel and I change clothes into my snow ninja suit and a backpack of the same color. Jordan is looking at me wide-eyed but remains silent.

"Come here babe, I need one last hug and kiss."

"Last?!"

"That's not what I meant. I'm applying my own poison to my fingernails and lips, and I wanted to feel you before doing so."

"Shit Mari that means his lips on yours."

"It might. I have to give him a false sense of security and I have to cover all possible outcomes. He has no clue who I am Jordan, but he'll get an idea when he sees what I'm wearing, which is more for exiting in case Lieu gets here before I'm ready. Give me your phone so I can text him."

Me: On my way, b there in 15

***

We pull up out of sight from the cabin and I go to get out. Jordan grabs my glove-covered hand to say, "Be careful." I place my hand on his cheek and look him in the eyes. "It'll be okay baby. This is what I do. Trust me."

"Trusting you isn't the problem."

"No worries love. I know Mack more than he thinks and I'm about to blow his world up . . . literally."

I get out of the car and walk to the cabin. I use my key to get in. I look to the living room and see Hank tied to a chair and

Mack jumping up to attention with wide eyes pointing his gun at me. I remove my facemask so Mack can see it's me and he actually looks happy to see me. He's so fucked up in the head; it's actually kinda sad.

"I'm here. Let Hank go. You alright Hank?" I ask as Mack cuts him loose.

"Yeah, I'm good." He says right before he starts for the door.

I keep my eyes on Mack when I tell Hank as he passes me, "When you get outside, go down the drive and down the hill. There's a car waiting for you there." Hank looks at me with concern and I wink at him to let him know it's okay. He leaves. "Ok Mack. You setup this meeting. Why?"

"Come on Mar. I haven't seen you in forever. I don't get a hug?"

"Really? Considering what I said to you the last time we talked, I'm surprised you want to see me at all. What happened to you Mack? This is not the guy I screwed the first night we met."

"Where's your friend?" he says through clenched teeth.

"I know you didn't go through all this to talk about him. What do you want Mack?"

"I want you and what the hell are you wearing?"

"Mack, haven't we had this discussion before? Don't I get to say who I want to be with?"

"I wanted another chance to convince you that we should be together."

"And you really thought grabbing Hank was the best way to do that?"

"Well it's not like you were going to let me get close to your boy toy, but I'm sure he's close by. I wonder how long I can keep you in here before he comes busting through that door."

I'm thinking the same damn thing.

JT

I see Hank coming down the hill to the car. He comes to the driver's side like he knows I won't leave. . .and he's right. I can't leave Mari behind.

"JT move over, I'll drive."

"No, I'm not leaving her!"

"JT, what's the plan?"

"Mari said once you got to me to go back to the motel."

"Ok makes sense because if she already alerted Lieu, Kam doesn't want us here when Lieu arrives. Move your ass, I'll drive!"

"Dammit Hank, NO! I will not leave her behind and she's got 10 minutes before I go in there. Now you can either get in the car out of the cold and wait with me or you can walk your ass back to the motel because I'M. NOT. LEAVING. HER!"

"Bruh, you sound like you're starting to lose it."

"Hank, how the fuck are you so calm?!"

"Well, considering what Kam did to me in my own backyard, how can I not have faith in her skills? I get it man. You love her and want to protect her but we both know she can actually take care of herself. You go in there and you may fuck everything up because she is not expecting you to get in the way."

"I can't just sit here!"

"JT, I don't think you get it. If you go in there, this will be your first encounter with someone who has a gun on you since your shooting. Add to the fact that it's the same person who actually shot you, and I can guarantee you, you are not ready to go in there. I think Kam knows that as well. You may think you're ready, and you might be, but from the way you are acting right now, I would suggest you keep your ass in this car and meet Kam back at the motel like she suggested."

"Hank, I have to go in there!"

"Ok, do what you feel you have to but I can tell you this . . . I wouldn't want to be on Kam's shit list if you both make it out unscathed!"

I think about it for a beat and I definitely wouldn't want to be on Mari's shit list, but I can't just sit here and wait. If she knows me, and I think she does, she has every expectation of me coming in there.

Kamari
Mack, do you think when I met you in that casino it was an accident?"

"I don't know, would it matter?"

"Do you ever wonder what happened to your coworker, Dwight?"

"No."

"I'm what happened to Dwight."

"What? What are you talking about?"

"Mack, I was originally hired to kill you for stealing from your boss, but my target changed to Dwight when you were cleared."

123

"Yeah right. Who sounds crazy now?"

"Mack, I'm gonna tell you a story and I want you to actually listen to what I'm saying." Mack sits down in the chair Hank was in previously and I hop up on the kitchen counter. "A couple of months ago, a hired killer received a notification to take out an employee who was thought to be stealing. This killer knew everything about this person necessary to find him and eliminate him quietly including where he lived and what he looked like. She followed him, finding him sitting at a roulette table in a Reno casino and struck up a conversation with him." At this point, Mack's facial expression is changing as my words seem to be sinking in. "The killer set out to have her way with him and then kill him, poisoning him with a delayed reaction where he could drive home and die alone, but the killer received another notification that her target was exonerated and replaced by another. The killer then decided to sleep with her mark anyway to get her rocks off and leave never to see him again."

"You're lying. That is the most ridiculous story I've ever heard."

"Does it matter? Unless I agree to give you what you want, you won't hear me anyway will you?"

"You're right, no matter what you say it doesn't matter unless you tell me we can be together. I've really missed you. Maybe next time I'll actually grab your boy toy so I can get him out of the way permanently. I bet you'll feel like talking to me then."

"Wow, you bring a whole new meaning to being 'pussy whipped'."

     I hear footsteps and I know exactly who they belong to. At this point, it almost seems like time slows. As the door opens, I slide my Gunsen fan made of Kevlar from my side holster. At the same time, Mack has a look of glee on his face when he sees who's opening the door and aims his gun to take a shot. Jordan also has his gun drawn, leading with it as he comes into the room. From Jordan's vantage point, he can't see me or Mack and the last thing I need is a gun fight. It'll be too messy a scene for when Lieu gets here, but what Jordan is doing was not unexpected. Before opening my fan, I strike Jordan's hand to make him drop the gun and right as I do that, Mack fires. I shake my Gunsen open protecting Jordan from the shot, then turn to throw several needles toward Mack. I grab Jordan by the collar and pull him down to the floor behind the kitchen island when I hear Mack's gun drop to the floor. I look at Jordan with more needles in my hand and ask him, "Do I need to use these on you to make you stay put?" He shakes his head no and he has a look in his eyes like he did when he was having nightmares, which is also something I was trying to avoid. "STAY. PUT." I stand up and walk over to Mack who is frozen, unable to move with beads of sweat on his forehead, breathing heavily, and looking right at me as I walk over to him. I get really close to his ear and speak softly. "Do you remember what I said I would do to you if I ever saw you again?" I move to his other ear by walking in front of him so he can see me. "I'm a woman of my word. It's your lucky day though as I really wanted to inflict some serious pain on you but I don't have the time." You can really see the fear in his eyes as I move around him, wondering what I'm going to do to him. Hmm, I only count four of the five needles thrown, one each in his forehead, hand (the one that was holding the gun), chest, and thigh. The fifth one is in rib of the back of the chair; it would have caught him in the balls if he wasn't in a standing motion when I threw them. SHIT, clearly I need more practice with moving targets. I pull the needle from the chair and place it at the base on the back of Mack's neck so the toxin can go directly into this spinal cord. He whimpers as I do so, then I push him down onto the chair and get to work, but first I need to check on Jordan.

Chapter 30

JT

I cannot even explain what happened. I walk into the cabin with my gun drawn and the next thing I knew, my gun is knocked out of my hand and I'm on the floor behind the island in the kitchen. I remember hearing the gunshot but don't remember getting hit or how I got to the floor. I do remember seeing Mari's murderous look telling me to stay put and yeah, I'm on her shit list. I hear someone walking toward me and I'm transported back into the nightmare I had so many times. SHIT, did he get to Mari, is he coming to finish me off. My breathing picks up until I see it's Mari coming back to check on me.

"Hey baby, let me check your wrist." She looks me over with what looks like hurt in her eyes. "It's bruised pretty bad, sorry but I had to make sure you would drop the gun. Hold this ice bag on it." She caresses my face when she says, "Look at me, stay here. I have stuff I need to finish and then we're leaving. Do not move from this spot. Understand me?"

All I could do is shake my head yes. It seemed like forever before Mari finally returned. She grabs me and tells me to come with her and we're out the door walking back to the car.

Kamari

I come back to the kitchen to check on Jordan and he seems to be having a panic attack. So I fix my face from the look I gave him earlier since the threat has been contained and I look at his wrist, which is banged up pretty bad. I have him hold the ice on it while I get everything else in order. I'm sure Lieu is on her way here now, so time is of the essence. I drew Mack's blood and placed the tube in my salad spinner to give it a whirl. After separating the plasma from the blood, I add it to the poison; I place that batch in my bag. I place pots on the stove with the unfinished poison, some of the Andromeda plants and a few small knives with the poison on their tips. I prick Mack's finger to make it look like he was in the process of making more poison and accidentally nicked himself with it before adding his own plasma, leading to him poisoning himself without his own barrier. I remove the needles from Mack and pick up the bullet casing; the bullet itself is lodged in my fan. By the time he starts to gain feeling back in his limbs, the poison will have done its work and will also eliminate any traces of the paralyzing toxin. I pull him to a standing position and push him face down on the couch, turning his head toward the table. I wipe down the living room and kitchen, anywhere I think Hank or Jordan has touched, and wash my hands and lips of my remaining poison and change gloves. I text Hank, because if Jordan is here, Hank didn't leave either.

"Baby, give me your phone."

> **Me: Hank pull up to the door and help me with Jordan**
> **Hank: Shit is he ok?**
> **Me: Physically yes, hurry up**

I open the front door so Hank doesn't have to grab the knob and when he arrives, he's looking around the room for Mack.

"Stop, the less you know the better. Help me get Jordan up and to the car. We need to go, now!"

We put Jordan in the back seat and I get back there with him. I have Jordan place his head between his legs and take deep breaths while I rub his back. I tell Hank to drive us back to the motel. I give him directions as I give him the rundown on what happened after he left me alone with Mack.

***

We pull up to the doors of our motel rooms and it seems like Jordan is coming back around. I tell Hank, "Do me a favor, go to that restaurant we passed on the way here and pick us up something to eat. You know what Jordan likes, get anything with fish or chicken for me. Here's your room key; you're right next door to us. I need to get Jordan on an even keel and we'll meet at your room for dinner, okay?"

"You got it sis. You sure you don't need any help, I've been there."

"How about this . . . after we all eat, I'll leave you two to talk. You can relate to him about this better than I can and he may share things with you he's not willing to share with me."

"I'll text you when I'm back in the room."

"Thanks Hank."

I grab Jordan by his good hand and pull him into our room. I start the shower. "Hey baby, how are you feeling?"

"I'm not sure. My wrist hurts and my head is kinda foggy."

"I'm sorry about your hand. Come on, let's get cleaned up and then we can eat, okay?"

"You mad at me babe? I know you told me to come back to the motel but I just couldn't, but I didn't help matters either, did I?"

"It's okay Jordan, everything worked out as planned. I even planned for you coming in after me. It's who you are. You staying behind meant Hank was close by as well. I needed his help to get you back here."

Jordan pulls me in for a hug, a hard one, almost to the point of pain but I get it. In that moment, he was back in his nightmares where Mack was taking me and finishing him off. All it took was the sound of that gun going off and he was done. I tried to shield him from that but I knew he wouldn't cooperate. I remove Jordan's and my clothes and walk him into the shower. I position him with his head under the water stream so the hot water can beat on the back of his neck while massaging his shoulders. I can feel the tension release from him as I do this. I soap his body and press firmly on his muscles to get him to relax. He turns to face me and I do the same to his front. It's like his body is one big stiff board. I shampoo his head, massaging his scalp, rubbing his temples, and he's finally starting to relax. He opens his eyes and looks like he's back. He's looking at me like he always does in these situations. I move him from under the water stream to the back of the shower and tell him "stay right there, don't move." I begin shampooing my own hair and washing my body, just to see how long he can watch without touching me. When I turn to face him after rinsing my front, I rinse the shampoo from my hair and that's when I feel his hot tongue on my right nipple. He stands up fully to help me squeeze the excess water from my hair and lifts me up. I wrap my legs around his waist and by the time we're against the back wall he's already inside me. He strokes me like he's making love to me for the first time as this will be a new beginning for us. With Mack out of the way, we can just live our lives together and I look forward to making those plans with him.

***

After several orgasms, we're dressing when I tell him, "Hey after we finish eating, I'm gonna leave you boys to talk. Clearly you have some things you need to get off your chest and I'm not the one you can do that with."

"Damn baby, you are the one I want to talk to about this. I just don't know how."

"I get it Jordan, but I think Hank is better equipped to help you with this; he's been there, and I'll be right here to share everything else. Okay?"

"You sure you're not mad at me for going against your wishes?"

"As long as you're not mad at me for fucking up your wrist. I'm still sick about that."

"We'll just call it even, but that look you gave me will haunt me for a bit."

"Sorry love. That face was never meant for you, but I had to make sure you knew I meant business, and the state of mind you were in, I couldn't talk to you in a normal tone. I had to be sure you followed my instructions from that point since you already disobeyed me."

"Disobeyed?"

"Yes?! Did I use the wrong word?"

"No ma'am."

"Good, let's eat."

Epilogue

Six months later

"Remember ladies, don't let the size of the guy make you feel you can't take him down. Everyone has a weakness, and when your adrenaline is flowing, you can move practically anything. When grabbed from behind,"—at this point, Jordan grabs me from behind still with a little bit of fear in his eyes after doing this for several weeks so we can demonstrate the move in slow motion. He's wearing full protective gear but I think it's adorable he's still apprehensive when it comes to these demonstrations, —"stump on his toe with your heel, push your hips back and to the side, then three hard strikes to the groin. Next week, I'll show you what to do if your attacker lifts you from behind, keeping you from stumping his foot but for now, who's going to show me what they've learned today against our lovely attackers?" Both Hank and Jordan come weekly to assist me with the women's self-defense class. The panic leaves their face when our attendees test out their skills, but when I demonstrate they look a little nervous as I can still hurt them through the protective gear. I'm still working on my restraint. I've had a lot of pent-up anger, so Sensei has me on a strict meditation schedule. Hank even got Lieu involved to give concealed weapons classes once a month. In another month, I'll begin teaching karate classes with some of the younger kids, so life has been pretty sweet, super busy, but great nonetheless.

Hank and Jordan are practically inseparable now, as Jordan still does his consulting on weird death cases but Hank is now his full-time partner. Every now and again Jordan will run some cases by me when it seems the killing is of an "assassin nature;" it keeps me on my toes.

A year later

       I return home from grocery shopping to find a box on the table next to my front door, which I have to say is really odd because I haven't needed one of my Sensei's packages in over a year and he has piqued my curiosity. When I step inside, the smells coming from the kitchen are wonderful and something I really love.

"Hey babe, whatcha cooking?"

"I have done a complete Japanese spread."

"Really? This is unexpected. What's the occasion?"

"It's all explained in the box from your Sensei. Open it up!"

Now I'm really curious. I open the box to find a letter and a small box underneath. I remove the letter, which reads:

> My Dearest Deshi,
>
> Over the past several months, your friend Jordan has been writing to me in order to get to know me since I'm your family. I was very touched by his high praise of you and humbled that he formally asked for your hand, which I gave without question. I take joy in knowing that you will no longer be alone as you live so far away and I'm excited to meet him in person on your trip here next month.
>
> Sensei

       When I look up from my letter with tears in my eyes, Jordan is on bended knee in front of me with the box from my package in his hand.

"Mari, you have no idea how long I have wanted to make you mine officially and I wanted to include your Sensei because I know he's practically your father. We collaborated on the design of your ring because I wanted it to include the things that are most important to you. You have no idea how much I love you and want to spend the rest of my life with you, and if you would do me the honor of becoming my wife, I will spend the rest of our days together making you happy."

When he opens the box, it's a ring made of platinum in the shape of a sai blade but it curves to wrap around my finger. There are four stones, two on each of the small points of the blade of my parents' birthstones (which are bent into the shape of a heart) and two diamonds to represent Jordan and myself on the middle blade where my parents' stones meet. It's beautifully done and the most thoughtful thing anyone has ever done for me. I'm so deep in thought and mesmerized by the ring, I don't realize I haven't answered Jordan.

"Babe, is it too much?"

"N-No, it's absolutely the most beautiful thing I have ever seen. Put it on me right this instant!"

It looks even better on my finger. "I'm never, ever taking this off . . . you know that right?"

"Is that a yes then?"

"Jordan, if you don't make me your wife, I will kill you in your sleep." I wink at him and pull him up so I can hug him . . . hard.

"I hope you don't mind but since you're not a traditional girl, I thought we can do a Japanese ceremony with your Sensei and we can do the reception when we return. Hank and Lieu will be tagging along for support, witnesses, and as close friends, of course."

"Hank and Lieu?"

"I know right. But ever since "the incident," they've been keeping in touch. Plus, with all the self-defense and concealed weapons classes, the four of us are around each other a lot. Hank has gone to Reno a few times and vice versa, and they've really hit it off.

"I'm happy for them, but you officially making me yours and marrying me at home in Japan with my Sensei present makes me happier than words can express. You are off to an excellent start Mr. Thompson."

"Well Mrs. Thompson, I aim to please. My Aunt Reyna will take care of the reception planning back East for our return. If you don't mind, we'll be in Japan for a month. We'll hang out with Hank and Lieu for a week, you with your Sensei for another week, and two weeks just for us."

"That sounds absolutely perfect!"

Author's Note

Thanks so much for reading Kamari and JT's story. We have truly enjoyed watching them come to life on the pages. I seriously considered a tragic ending leaving Kamari alone in the world again but my daughter vehemently begged me not to be *that* author. Of course, I was influenced by most of the stories I have read the past year and a half and they all have a happy ending but we know sometimes life does not always work out that way. For some reason, I wanted her to end up alone after having someone really care for her and turn into a cold-blooded killer not needing the money as motivation. C'est la vie.

Don't forget to leave your review about the book. We truly appreciate you taking the time to purchase and read this series. Please take the time to do your review and share with others what you thought of them. Your reviews are THE BEST advertisement and we as authors cannot sell books without you, the readers!

Our next book is out of the mind of my daughter. She's a SciFi fan, so this one will be more of a YA-SciFi fantasy book but trust me, the adults will love it too. Be on the lookout.

We want to hear from you. We are on FaceBook, Twitter and Instagram at JnLBrownBooks. You can follow us there for book release dates and special offers. You can also email us at JnLBrownBooks@gmail.com.